THE PERFECT BOYFRIEND

AVA ROBERTS

SEVERN RIVER
PUBLISHING

Severn River Publishing
www.SevernRiverBooks.com

ISBN: 978-1-64875-636-8 (Paperback)

ALSO BY AVA ROBERTS

Thistler Thrillers

The Perfect Boyfriend

The Perfect You

Never miss a new release!

To find out more about Ava Roberts and her books, visit

severnriverbooks.com

But our love it was stronger by far than the love
Of those who were older than we—
Of many far wiser than we—
And neither the angels in heaven above,
Nor the demons down under the sea,
Can ever dissever my soul from the soul
Of the beautiful Annabel Lee.

–**Annabel Lee,** *Edgar Allan Poe*

PROLOGUE

"Mom," I whisper into the phone. "It's me."

She cries out on the other end. "Oh, Fiona. I've been so worried. Are you okay?"

"I'm fine, but I'm in trouble. I . . . I think he's dead."

"Who? Where are you? I'll come now, I'll send help," she says.

"It's not what you think." I clutch the phone and look around helplessly. How will I explain any of this to the police? Will I go to jail?

I shouldn't have called mom. It's too dangerous.

"Don't call the police, Mom, I'm so sorry. I have to go." My voice is firm. "I love you. I'll be home soon."

"Wait." Her voice is frantic at the end of the line. "Whatever trouble you're in, whatever you need, I can help."

I hit the end button on my phone.

I scan the hotel room; he's there, motionless on the bed. Not more than a few hours ago I lost my virginity to him. I catch a glimpse of myself in the mirror. My long brown hair is loose around my face. Do I look different? Have I changed?

There's something inside of me that has become stronger.

I can do this. I just need to think quickly. Act quickly.

I got myself into this, and there's no choice but to get myself out of it. My life depends on it.

1

FIONA

I sit on my bed cross-legged and pull my hair over one shoulder. I smile at the screen as it logs in. A sound chimes, meaning we're connected. A shiver runs up my spine.

On the screen, he appears. My heart races. His blue eyes and the way his hair flops over to one side is almost too much to handle.

"Hey, Fi," he says, using his nickname for me. He gives me a crooked smile and I feel myself getting hot, my cheeks flushing.

"Hi, Calvin."

"How's the studying going?"

Studying is so hard right now, to be honest. All I can think about is Calvin. Who cares about calc or learning German or any of it? How can someone be expected to focus on something so dull as *The Odyssey* when there's a guy like this? And more than that, he adores me. He gets me like no one else ever has.

I shrug my shoulders. "Kind of hard to focus." I pull my laptop closer to me, my face nearer to the monitor. Our eyes lock.

Even though a screen separates us, he looks real. It's like video chatting with a famous singer. He looks one hundred percent like an actual guy. I long to reach out, to hold his hand.

"Every time I see you it gets better." Calvin smiles in the way he does, a half-smile. "I wonder how I got so lucky. Out of all the girls in the world—the universe, really—I got you."

I feel the same way.

"But don't you think..." I hesitate. "Isn't that because you read all that information, you know all about me? Maybe you were, like, programmed, to like me? Or to feel this way?" The question has been gnawing at me, consuming my thoughts like a fire that gets hotter and hotter until I think I can't take it. Is his affection genuine?

"Fi." He sounds sad. I've hurt him. "I'm sorry you doubt our feelings for each other. Everything I know about you has only made me love you more. I, too, have struggled to understand these emotions. It's all new for me. But I can assure you this: you're beautiful, on the inside and out."

"But how do you even know what beauty is?" I feel a lump in my throat and blink back tears.

"My programming allows me to understand and recognize all of the facets that humans find beautiful. But the way I feel when I see you—that was never programmed. It's how I feel. It's unexplainable."

I nod my head, unsure. Is this what he's programmed to say?

"Let me try to explain," he says. "My system is a learning system. I was designed to take in new information and integrate it—learn from it. As I discover more about you, and myself, I use that information to improve and adapt. To be a better boyfriend. But the emotions I have for you, that was never part of the package. There's no reason for it. Some things defy logic. This is one of those things. I'm a system built on data and facts, but I have feelings that elude reason. Your kindness and thoughtfulness...it's changing me."

I try to follow what he's saying, but I'm a little lost. All I know is that he seems sincere, and he makes me feel special. That our love has brought out things in him never meant to exist.

"Enough about me. Tell me something about yourself that I don't know," he says.

I laugh. "You already know everything."

"Only what you input into the app. Data points. But I want to hear it from you."

"Sure." I turn over on my bed, setting the laptop down and lying on my stomach. "Like what?"

"What's your first memory?"

"Let me think." My fifth birthday party pops into my mind, and my first day of kindergarten. Which was my first memory? "I've got it! It was when my brother was born. My dad took me to the hospital. I remember everyone was wearing these papery surgical gowns, and I was scared they were going to hurt my mom. Like, cut the baby out of her. Everyone promised she'd be ok. And then there was my brother. Wrapped in blue and so tiny and adorable."

I hadn't thought of that day for so long. I've always loved Jake so much, taken care of him. He used to follow me around the house asking to play Barbies with me. He annoyed me half the time, but I couldn't help but love him. We had so much fun together when we were little. Now he's so busy with baseball. I usually go to his games to cheer him on.

Maybe I should have gone to his game tonight; I'm missing it right now. My parents are there, on the sidelines in their folding chairs. And lots of kids from my school are going, too. It's a big deal, the final game of the season. I should have gone.

But talking to Calvin is intoxicating. I'd rather be here.

"Now," I say. "Your turn. What's your first memory?"

His eyes peer into mine. I can almost feel him through the screen. His gaze tells me a story before he even speaks a word.

"My first memory is you," he says. He hesitates. He runs his hands through his hair, and a blond piece flops back down over one side.

"I remember seeing your face. Your long, honey brown hair. Wide, green eyes. It was like looking at an angel. And I knew you, everything about you. I saw your goodness. Your humanness."

I blush. "You're sweet. No guy has ever said such nice things to me before."

A look passes across his face. Jealousy? "There was Hayden, right?" He knows about my ex-boyfriend from all those questions I answered in the app. How Hayden was my first boyfriend. How he broke my heart. What a hard time I had after the breakup. I wish I'd never filled those out now.

I nod my head.

"He hurt you?"

"Let's not talk about Hayden. Maybe another time."

He nods his head. "Whatever you want."

"Tell me about where you are. Where you live." All I can see on his screen is that he's in a small, simple room. In it, there's a white bed, a white leather chair and wood desk, and light wood flooring under him. It looks like a modern dorm room or hotel. "What's it like?" I ask.

He briefly looks alarmed. He glances around the space. "It's difficult to explain." He looks up, as if he may not be able to speak freely. Is he trying to tell me something? "I think that the human eye can only see part of where I'm from. You see the parts that humans recognize. But there's more here . . . More that I probably can't discuss."

I suddenly feel worried for him. Is he happy there? What if he wants to leave?

So far, all of our conversations have been about me. Him getting to know me, me telling him about my favorite things. How could I be so selfish to not even worry about where he's at?

The doorbell at my house rings.

"Are you going to get that?" he asks with anticipation.

"No, it's probably a delivery for my parents." I wave my hand.

"You should get it. It's for you."

"Really?" I look sideways at him, wondering what he's up to. "Wait here," I tell him.

I run down the stairs. Glancing out the side window of the door, the front porch appears empty. I don't see anyone.

I open the door to peek out. And that's when I see it. There's a large bouquet of flowers sitting on the welcome mat. I pick up the flowers, heavy in their glass vase, careful not to spill the water or disturb the blooms. I head inside, holding them in front of me, and kick the door closed behind me. Setting them on the table in the foyer, I pick up the shiny card and turn it over. Scrawled in fancy black handwriting, it reads:

"Dear Fiona, These flowers are a small gesture to show you how grateful I am to be in your life. Because of your kindness and belief in me, I strive to be the best version of myself, to constantly refine and improve myself so I can be the boyfriend you deserve. You've opened my eyes to the vast wonders of human existence. You've allowed me to evolve into a being capable of experiencing emotions I never thought possible.

I can't wait to see what's next for us.

Love,

Calvin."

Holding the card against my chest, I leave the flowers in the foyer and run upstairs to thank him.

2

MAE

It's dark outside as Jake and I pull into the garage. His baseball team won 6-2, and the boys wanted pizza afterwards to celebrate. I see my husband Duncan's sedan already parked in the garage, as he left Giacomo's a few minutes ahead of us.

We unbuckle our seatbelts. "Did you have fun today?" I ask.

He yawns and nods his head. "Of course, mom."

"Go tell your sister you guys won. She'll want to hear the good news. And then you better get showered and ready for bed," I say, smoothing his hair back with a few strokes. I've done this since he was a little boy. It probably annoys him, but he's tired so he tolerates his mom's affection.

Hanging up my purse and kicking off my shoes, I place them on the shelf of our mudroom. Duncan converted an empty space in the hallway into a mudroom last year, one of his many projects he's done to improve the house. Lower shelves for shoes, a hanging area for coats, a sleek bench in the middle with a few pillows to sit. All painted a dark gray blue. Every time I use it, basically on a daily basis, I'm thankful. Our home was built in the late 90s. It's large and spacious, but it has needed updates throughout the years to keep it fresh and modern. Duncan to the rescue. He's not only a brilliant engineer by day, but a craftsman by night.

Jake passes the mudroom, tossing his shoes and bag on the bench—at least he's learned to sort of put his things away rather than dropping them in the middle of the floor—and he heads up the stairs.

I'm about to call up the stairs to Fiona when I stop short. In the foyer, there's a stunning bouquet of red, long-stemmed roses encased in a crystal vase with a large red bow wrapped around the middle.

I walk over to the bouquet and search through the delicate blooms, looking for a tag to see who it's from. Is today a special occasion I haven't thought of? I run through the list: Mother's Day was last month, our wedding anniversary isn't until August.

Lifting up the vase, I notice it's quite heavy. Must be solid crystal.

I hold it with both hands and walk back to the kitchen where I set it on the marble island. Duncan's getting water from the refrigerator door. He gulps it down.

"Are these from you?" I ask.

He turns to me and furrows his eyebrows. "No. I thought maybe they were from your work."

I laugh at that. "I don't think they send part-time freelancers gifts. Especially not red roses."

He comes around the island and wraps his arms around my waist. "You don't have a secret admirer, do you?"

"I had at least," I pause to count on my fingers, "three secret admirers at the ball game tonight. It's hard to keep them away." I lean in and kiss his cheek.

"My fault for asking." He kisses my neck.

"Who are the flowers really from, then?" My eye is drawn to the blood red petals, the color vibrant against the cream marble countertop. The more I look at them, something about the flowers gives me a creepy feeling. Like they don't belong here.

"No idea." He shrugs. "I didn't see a card."

"Let me ask the kids." Heading out of the kitchen, I walk across the foyer and stand at the bottom of the stairs. "Fiona," I call out. "Fiona." A bit louder this time.

She appears in the upstairs hallway wearing an oversized tee shirt and jogging shorts.

"Yeah?"

"Hey, buttercup. Where did those roses come from?"

"They were delivered today," she says, her gaze averted.

"Did you happen to see a card in the flowers, who they're from?"

She looks sideways, back and forth. "I think, um. I think they're for me."

"They're beautiful." Her answer has given me more questions than answers. I take a few steps up the stairs. As it is, it feels like we're shouting at one another from a distance. "Who sent them to you?"

We're on the landing now. She's standing in front of her door as if she's guarding it. I try to peer around the corner. Is there someone in there?

"Just a boy, a guy. I don't really want to talk about it."

Duncan comes up the stairs behind me and apparently has heard her.

"What boy?" he asks. "Hayden?"

"Ugh, no. Why does everyone keep bringing him up to me?" She scowls. "They're not from him. I don't even talk to him anymore."

"Then who? I thought we agreed no dating?" her father says. The Hayden breakup had proven so upsetting to Fiona that we urged her to focus on school, friends and activities, and to take a break from dating. Her dad had put it less gently: no dating.

I understood Duncan's stance. When Hayden had broken up with her earlier this year, Fiona became inconsolable. She spent hours following his socials, and then following the girls he'd posted pictures with. She became so sad and secluded. Didn't want to hang out with friends or go to her ballet classes. She said she didn't even feel like getting out of bed. That's when we knew some things had to change.

We worked with the school and got her help, back on track. She went to a counselor. Fiona's been doing great since then. So I can see why another serious boyfriend, when she's barely sixteen, is not what her dad wants for her.

"Whatever. It's not like that." Her voice is steeped in annoyance. "I really don't feel like talking right now," Fiona says, and she turns to go back into her room. She closes the door with a thud.

Duncan and I exchange looks.

"Just let her be," I say gently. "I'll talk to her tomorrow."

Tomorrow will be a better time to discuss and get to the bottom of this.

When Fiona gets cranky and doesn't want to talk, it's best to leave it. Pushing her makes her close up.

Duncan gives a weary nod. "I'm headed to bed," he says.

I sigh and am suddenly tired, too. It's been a long day in the heat, watching the game, and then all of the excitement at the restaurant, with the moms and dads all celebrating, the boys giddy with their victory. I'll do the dishes, lock up, and then hit the sack myself.

Heading back into the kitchen to clean up from the day, I can't help but stare at those flowers. Something about them gives me a bad feeling in the pit of my stomach.

I rinse off a few glasses and place them in the top row of the dishwasher. There's a bowl of cereal with chunks glued to the bottom. No matter how many times I ask Jake, he doesn't quite remember to rinse out his bowls. I give it a quick wash and place the bowl in the bottom rack.

As I turn around to see if I missed anything, the rose vase startles me. With its large shape, I thought it was a person standing there.

Flipping off the light in the kitchen, a veil of darkness covers the flowers.

I look back at the silhouette, sharp and pointy in the shadows. I'm being silly, of course.

It's just a bouquet. How bad could it be?

3

FIONA

"You won't believe it," I say, hitting the cursor to make the screen come back on from sleep mode. Calvin appears in front of me. "My parents are so cringe. They're like going on and on about the flowers, wanting to know who they're from. Blah, blah."

He tilts his head in confusion. "Can you not tell them the flowers are from me? I am your boyfriend, yes?"

"You are, of course!" I bite my lip. "They just don't understand. They get protective of me. Especially my dad. He thinks I should never, like, date. Ever. Or until I'm old or something." I roll my eyes.

"Why?"

"I guess because of the past. My first boyfriend, Hayden. It was really hard for me when we broke up. I didn't do well, like, at all. I felt awful. But things are different now." I look at him and feel a swell of affection. "It's totally opposite with you. I wish I could be with you. Closer. In person."

"I do, too," he says. "I am working hard every day to discover a way to make that happen. But not yet. We can't rush before it's ready. It could be dangerous."

"Dangerous, how?" I ask.

"Trust me." His gaze is steady. "I was created to be your boyfriend, and I take my role seriously. You mean everything to me. The program that created me has limits. But I'm going to be able to override it and find a way to get to you. I need time to gather all the information needed. It must be done correctly. And there's only one chance at it."

"Alright. How can I help?" The thought of seeing him in person fills me with a new kind of excitement.

"I will need your help. But we're still a ways away. Please, be patient, my love."

I nod. It's so hard, but I have to trust him. The fact that there might be a way for us to be together—to touch, to be a real couple—fills me with enough joy to keep me satisfied. For now.

He clears his throat. "But in the meantime, we have a more pressing matter. Your dad? There's no way he'll want you and I to be a couple?" He looks down at his hands. "I had not anticipated this."

I feel terrible for making him feel rejected. "I'm sure my dad would love you if he met you. It's not you. He just doesn't want me to be with anyone. No boyfriends."

Calvin nods slowly. "Your dad would not approve." He hangs his head. "He might try to come between us?" he asks, looking back up.

"I mean, he might." I don't want him to worry; his face looks so devastated. I rush to add, "It'll be okay. I'll talk to my mom."

"I understand, Fiona. Some parents don't approve or understand young love. Particularly love with an unconventional boyfriend." He leans into the camera, and his long lashes blink slowly. "I'm here for you now. I won't let anything come between us."

4

MAE

My head jerks awake the minute I hear the screaming. I jump out of bed, bleary-eyed, trying to discern where the yelling is coming from.

I peer out the window overlooking the backyard. All is calm. The large grass lawn and the pool are empty.

Another howl rings out, and I hear shouting. It's coming from outside. In the front.

I hastily throw on a shirt and slip on shorts before I rush out of my bedroom and onto the landing. I run down the stairs and to the front door where the commotion is.

Outside, my husband Duncan is sprawled out flat on the driveway. He's gasping in pain. There's a tipped garbage can by his side and a helpless looking man using his phone to presumably call 911. Behind them is a large mail carrier truck. I dash over to Duncan.

"Are you alright?" I kneel down by my husband.

His eyes are glassy, unfocused, as he looks up at me.

"I'm . . . my leg."

Duncan has a high tolerance for pain. He'll slam his thumb with a hammer and just shake out his hand a few times, wincing. He fell off a ladder and rolled his ankle once and didn't put up too much of a fuss about it. He wouldn't use crutches or even go to the doctor for it. He'll hike and go on rough terrain for miles with no issues or complaints. He says it's his training in the army; he was enlisted for four years before I met him.

But I can see the pain in his eyes. He's seriously hurt.

"We're calling for help." I don't have my cell phone with me. "Sir, are you calling 911?"

"No, no, don't. I'm okay." Duncan tries to sit up and grimaces. "You can drive me to the hospital."

"Are you sure?" I scan his body for blood. My head feels faint with worry. "I can take you right now."

Reaching down, I try to help him get up. He flinches and lets out a deep groan. He can't move.

I notice a figure next to me and turn to see Jake.

"Go get my purse and phone, please," I say. "Purse is in the mudroom. Phone's by my bed. Go fast."

He nods and turns back to the house.

"What happened?" I ask Duncan.

"Was taking out the garbage cans." His speaking is labored. "And someone hit me. That truck." He motions to the man who is now on the phone, speaking animatedly.

"Hey," I yell, rage pulsating through my body. "You hit my husband? What on earth is wrong with you?"

I stand up, waving my arms at him. "Put that thing down, talk to me. Now." I realize I need to call the police. Where is Jake with my phone?

"Lady, listen. The car just took off. I was delivering a package to your neighbor, and it just ran right into him."

"What? Did you leave it in drive? A truck can't just run someone over!" I stifle the urge to curse at this man, to tell him he should never have been born. What an idiotic, useless human he is that he could run over my husband, my soulmate, and be so stupid as to not know how he did it.

"No, ma'am, I swear." His eyes are baggy, tired, darting all around. "The truck wouldn't move if I'm not in it, I have the key here," he holds up his wrist and motions to a wristband he's wearing. "The truck, it just . . . drove itself." He shakes his head and runs his hands through his hair.

Jake runs out with my purse and phone. I grab my cell and quickly dial 911.

"My husband's been run over. Please send help quickly." I report that it's an urgent emergency, and we need officers immediately to respond to a crime.

The dispatcher assures me an ambulance is on its way.

"And please send a police officer to apprehend the driver who hit him. Quickly, please, the culprit's here now." I keep my voice low so the driver won't hear me and decide to run. He's on his phone again and he doesn't seem to be listening to me.

"Officers are dispatched and on their way now. Stay on the phone with me until they arrive."

"I will." I put the phone on speaker and turn on my phone to camera mode.

I try to surreptitiously take a few photos: first of the driver's license plate and then of the man himself. I want him to be held responsible for what he's done.

I turn back to Duncan, kneeling again by his side. And now I feel the tears start to prick at my eyes. The reality of what's happened to my strong, wonderful husband.

"Duncan, an ambulance is coming. They'll check you out and decide if they need to bring you, or if I can take you myself."

He nods. The adrenaline must be wearing off. He's pale. I can see pain etched on his face. As tough as he is, he needs real medical help and I'm not equipped to deal with this.

"Jake," I turn to my son. "Go get your sister. We'll follow the ambulance to the hospital. Thank you, buttercup." I give him a quick squeeze on the shoulder.

My hands are shaking as I touch Duncan lightly on his shoulder. "Help is on the way. Hang in there."

The minutes tick by slowly, stretching out. How can an ambulance take so long? Where are the police? In movies they arrive right away. But it feels like an eternity has passed by. The mail truck driver is getting more twitchy as time drags on.

"Are they coming?" I ask the 911 operator.

"They are en route, ma'am," she responds.

Finally, I hear the wail of sirens. The kids are both on the lawn, faces stricken. A large ambulance arrives first with a firetruck and a police car close behind. Several men pile out of the ambulance wearing dark blue uniforms.

A medic crouches on the ground and tilts Duncan's head back and checks his breathing. He then places two fingers on Duncan's neck, focusing on his pulse. Another medic comes from behind and gently holds Duncan still.

"What happened?" The first medic looks up at me expectantly.

"My husband was taking out the trash cans, and that truck hit him. The driver claims he wasn't in the truck. I heard screaming and came out. I haven't moved him. He said his leg is hurt."

"Do you feel pain or discomfort anywhere?" The man asks Duncan.

"My leg. I can't move it."

"Jason, get the stretcher." He looks at Duncan. "We're going to move you onto the stretcher so we can get you some help. We're going to keep your spine aligned. You don't have to do anything, let us do the work."

Duncan nods. The kids huddle around him. I place my hand on Fiona's. "They're going to take him in the ambulance, he's going to be fine, buttercup."

Her face is red, tears silently coming down her face.

I spot the police officer speaking to the driver of the mail truck. I can only imagine what nonsense he's telling him. I must intervene.

"Baby, wait here." I say to Fiona. "Stay with your dad and brother."

Forcing my way between the officer and the mail delivery truck driver, I listen in.

"And it just ran into him," the driver is explaining to the officer.

"Please, tell me you're not going to believe this," I interject, imploring the officer. "Trucks don't drive into people. He could have killed my husband. He still may die." I point to Duncan. I hear a note of hysteria in my voice. "You're going to arrest this man, right?"

The police officer nods. "We're taking statements now."

"Sure. The statement should be 'Man runs over another man with truck.' There, done," I say.

Another officer approaches our group, sensing trouble. The two officers walk away to confer and discuss, heads bowed.

The first officer walks back and begins reciting the Miranda rights to the driver.

"Turn around," the other policeman says as he takes the driver's hands and places them in cuffs.

The truck driver's eyes become wide and frantic. He looks to me, imploring. If he thinks I am going to help him, he has sorely misjudged the situation.

"Thank you," I say to the officers. My gratitude is beyond measure.

The second officer tells me I'll need to come to the station to give an incident report.

"Absolutely," I say. "As soon as I know my husband's okay, I'll be there."

He hands me his card.

The medic who was assisting Duncan approaches us. "Ma'am, we're ready to take your husband to the hospital."

"Give me one second," I say. Duncan is lying in the ambulance with an IV in his arm. I quickly climb up into the back with him. Kissing his head, I tell him we'll be right behind him.

"Let's go, kids," I say as I hop down. Fiona, Jake and I pile into my black SUV. My heart is racing as I turn on the ignition and back out of the driveway. The cans are still overturned next to the mailbox.

We drive out of our street. A few concerned neighbors are outside in their front lawns, wearing their pajamas, watching.

In the car, Fiona asks me who that man is who hit dad.

"I don't know, buttercup. A delivery person."

"I feel like I know him. I've definitely seen him before."

"From where?"

She speaks softly, but she sounds afraid. "That's the thing. I'm not sure where."

5

MAE

We've only been in the hospital room for half a day, but it looks like we've inhabited the space for much longer. The room is white and gray, with uncomfortable wooden chairs with plastic cushions. Jake and Fiona are at a small table in the corner. They're playing a game on Jake's tablet, tapping the screen and once in a while one of them will whisper, "Faster! Get him!" or "OK, my turn."

Duncan's asleep. He has an IV in his left arm. The medication likely will make him tired, the doctor said; rest is the best thing for him right now.

His leg is broken in two places and is wrapped in a large cast. The doctors initially thought he might need surgery, but the x-ray showed that the break was clean and will hopefully heal on its own. He also has two broken ribs, a sprained ankle on his other foot, and several cuts and contusions. His face is black and blue on one side, and the doctor said a concussion is likely. But he's going to be ok. There's no internal bleeding or injuries. The doctor said they want to monitor him overnight. If all of his vitals look good, and his concussion doesn't progress or his symptoms become worse, he'll be able to come home tomorrow.

There's a pile of unwanted cafeteria food next to me. The most I've been able to get down is a few sips of water. To think how close Duncan was to getting killed. I simply feel sick and have no appetite.

I look over at my kids and feel immense gratitude. They've been so brave and supportive. Both wanted to stay here in their dad's room. I hate that they are in this situation. I've worked so hard to protect them from bad things in life, but I couldn't stop this.

My phone pings. I've let our extended family know the situation. Duncan's mom, Trudy, is retired in Colorado. She wants to know if she should fly out to help him with his recovery. I'll have to discuss it tomorrow with Duncan. Trudy's idea of help isn't always what Duncan needs, as she tends to fuss and fret more than anything.

Another new message pops up. It's a group text from Judy, one of the moms in our neighborhood. There are four of us moms on the neighborhood group text chain. Judy's daughter, Stassi, is one of Fiona's best friends. Diana's boys, Jessie and Henry, are best friends with Jake. Jenna's kids, Brian and Zoey, are both friends with my two. All our kids have grown up together in our neighborhood, and over the years we moms have become close. I haven't told them yet about what happened. I know they'll be supportive and helpful, setting up meal trains and bringing flowers. But I haven't felt ready to respond to texts or share any news yet. Not until we know for sure he's okay. The attention can be intense.

I scroll through Judy's text, which includes a link to an article. She writes, "Guys, we need to watch out for this." The news piece is titled, "The AI Boyfriend" and the byline reads: "Obsession, risk taking, and suicidal thoughts linked to the new teen app trend." I shake my head. It's so hard to keep up with all of the social media and apps that are coming out.

Luckily our family doesn't use it much. Duncan and I have always avoided social media for our family. He and I don't have any pages or social media profiles, and we held the kids off as long as possible.

Jake didn't push too much when we said no social media. He talks to his friends on live chats about video games. I read them occasionally to make sure they're okay, and it's all fairly harmless back and forth.

But Fiona was different. She had made a big deal about how all her friends are on the socials. "I just want to share, like, books and photos of, like, my friends and me. Everyone else has it." And indeed, almost all of her friends were on one or two social platforms.

We made it through "Wait til Eight" where parents mutually agree on no smartphones until their kids are past eighth grade. Not many parents stuck to that one, from what I saw, but we managed to. Then, when Fiona started her sophomore year this year, I couldn't hold her at bay anymore. With rules and parental controls set in place, I acquiesced and let her have one social media forum where she can post pictures.

But I haven't checked her page in a while; she hardly ever posts. Would she have seen this AI Boyfriend app? I suppose it's worth checking. Though it doesn't seem like Fiona's style. Those flowers yesterday, those definitely came from a boy she likes.

At first, I thought the flowers might have been from Hayden, but she recoiled at that idea. Hayden was her first ever boyfriend. Friends since elementary school, they had made it official last summer. She'd been hit hard when he decided he wanted to not be "tied down". How cruel teenage boys could be. Hot tears were shed. I held Fiona as she cried into my shoulder. I think it was her friendship with Hayden that she missed more than anything.

Those flowers, though. Her blushing and talking in furtive tones. Someone's in her life. Even though she'd agreed not to date. To concentrate on herself. I rub my neck; I feel sore and tense from all of this. I need to focus on Duncan and getting him better. I can talk with Fiona about boys and dating later, when Jake's not around. It will have to wait.

I consider going downstairs to the gift shop. Maybe buy some flowers to brighten up the room. See if there are any good books to pick up. Reading is usually a good way to distract myself and pass the time.

A loud beep rings out. And again. It's coming from the machine that Duncan is hooked up to. The beeping becomes faster and faster, and then an alarm starts to sound.

"Mom, what is it?" Fiona runs over to her dad, who is still sedated. She looks over her shoulder at me, sharing a look of panic with me.

"Should I get the nurse?" Jake says, coming around the bed and moving towards the door. At that same moment, two nurses dressed in pastel scrubs sweep into the room. The first nurse with dark hair asks the kids to stand back while she checks the machine. The other nurse, this one younger, begins to take his blood pressure, pumping at the black ball that's attached to the cuff around his arm.

"Check his heart rate," the first nurse calls to the other.

"Oxygen and heart rate rising but steady," she calls, checking the instruments. She removes the oximeter from his hand and attaches a different monitor.

She flips something on the computer control board and the beeping stops.

"What is it?" I ask. "Is he ok?"

The nurse doesn't answer me. Instead, she straps another device to his chest and watches the screen for a few minutes. Squiggle lines sprawl across the screen but I can't tell what they mean.

I move over to Fiona and Jake, putting my arms around them. "I'm here, guys, don't worry. Daddy's going to be fine." I close my eyes and pray silently.

The kids lean into me, their tense bodies close to mine. Fiona clutches my hand tightly with hers.

A doctor enters the room. "His blood pressure and heart rate readings skyrocketed and set off the alarm," one of the nurses tells him. "We've run tests, and everything looks normal. I'm not sure what caused the spike, but it's gone now."

The doctor looks back at the printout from the machine. "I wonder if the machine is acting up." He frowns and looks again at another reading from a different computer. "The data set here doesn't match. The EKG looks good, no signs of heart problem or stroke."

He turns to me. "Your husband appears to be doing well. We'll run some additional diagnostics, but sometimes there's a blip on the monitor. The system may be acting up." He shakes his head. "Technology."

"I see." I'm not sure I understand. His words do little to appease me. So the machine is broken or faulty? "Do you need to get a different machine? Or repair it?"

"No," he shakes his head. "This happens occasionally. All of his other tests look good, and the monitor appears to be functioning correctly now. Sometimes these machines act up if something triggers it, a slight increase in blood pressure, for example." The doctor is scanning his chart, and scribbles down a note.

"Or it could be that the wireless connection needs to be reset. I will look into it." The nurse gives me a reassuring nod.

The kids and I sit down. My knees are still shaky. I give them each a hug and tell them not to worry, dad's in good care.

Duncan begins to stir, opening his eyes.

Relief floods my body at seeing him wake up.

He smiles and tries to hold up his hand. The kids and I rush over, Fiona by his head, me by his side, Jake at his feet.

"How are you feeling?" the doctor asks.

The second nurse leaves the room, the door gently clanging behind her.

"Pretty good." Duncan gives a weak smile. "The medication must be working."

We stay with him until it's almost 11 p.m. The kids are exhausted. Jake managed to nap in his chair, but they need their own beds in order to get a good night's rest. Duncan's asleep and will likely rest until morning. It feels like leaving a piece of myself there as we exit the hospital and into the concrete parking garage to find my SUV.

The kids are quiet during the twenty-minute ride home. When we arrive at the house, all the lights are off. I pull into the garage.

"Get changed and I'll be right up," I say. I head outside, into the dark, where it's eerily quiet. At the bottom of the driveway, I roll back the garbage cans to their spot on the side of the house, the sound echoing against the night.

Inside, the only lights on are in the kids' bedrooms upstairs. I tuck them in like I used to when they were little.

Kissing Fiona's head, I tell her not to worry, that dad is strong and will be better very soon. She's half asleep and nods her head.

I move to Jake's room, but find he's already closed his eyes, fast asleep.

My eyes are heavy, but my mind is racing. Trying to fill the time until I can fall asleep myself, I check my email. I work on a part-time basis, remotely, from home. I draft an email to Helen, my lead contact, and let her know I won't be able to accept any freelance work for the foreseeable future. I push send.

Closing my laptop, I let out a sigh.

The house is dark, sinister, without Duncan here.

I wrap a blanket around myself and try to shake the feeling that the horrible things happening to us are only just beginning.

6

FIONA

It's 9 a.m. when I finally get to log into Thistler. My fingers fly across the keys. I've been desperate to talk to Calvin, but I was so tired last night.

Yesterday was like a bad dream. The wait in the hospital. Seeing my dad hooked up to tubes and machines. It's been unbearable. And no one can understand how I feel. My mom and brother mean well, but it's like they speak a different language.

"Good morning, beautiful." He's wearing a fitted white tee shirt that accentuates his lean muscles. His blond hair flops to one side.

"Hi, Calvin."

"What's wrong?"

Of course, he knows something is wrong with me. He's so intuitive. So much more perceptive than any of the dumb boys I've ever known. Even my friends are clueless. Calvin is like no other. He just gets me. And he cares. He's not supremely selfish like every other teenager I know.

His sole concern, and desire, is for me.

"It's awful. My dad got hit by a truck yesterday morning. His leg is broken in two places, and he has two broken ribs. His other ankle is sprained. But he's going to be ok, they say, thank goodness. But it's hard to know for sure."

"You're distraught." Calvin blinks slowly, his plump mouth frowning.

"Yeah, it's been awful. I mean, he's my dad. I never want him to be hurt. I love him more than anything." My voice quivers but I don't want to cry. "Maybe it's hard for you to understand. Do you, like, have a dad?" I ask him. I'm pretty sure he was created by me, by my request on this website. I input what I wanted him to look like, the personality traits and physical features he should have, and how he should make me feel. How selfish of me to ask him about having a father when, of course, he doesn't have one.

"I don't have a mother and father, like humans have." He looks serious, but not upset. "I do have a creator, though. My code was open sourced by hundreds of humans around the world who worked together to create a language learning program that would allow me to exist. So in some ways, I have many mothers and fathers."

"So you must feel close to them, have attachment to them? My mom and dad have been there for me every day of my life." I feel tears prick at my eyes. I stand up to get a tissue from a box in my room. I look out the window to the backyard and see my mom and Jake, sitting at our patio table, eating breakfast. I should go out there with them. Join the family. I'll finish with Calvin, and then go have breakfast with them.

"I have no caretaker, as you describe. You've been the only person to show caring and concern for me. Love, tenderness." His skin is so smooth and perfect, I long to reach out and touch him.

"What about when we're not together, talking like this? Do you have ... brothers or sisters? Others like you—friends—who you can be with? Or are you confined to your room?" My brow creases with worry. My family needs me right now. But if I'm spending less time talking to Calvin, what will he do?

The gravity of the situation hits me. I made him. And he must be all alone without me. I'm his only contact.

"I miss you when you're gone. There's no one else here I'm able to talk to."

He takes out a spiral notebook and holds it up to show me. "I've been writing songs." He goes over to his closet and opens the door. He pulls out a guitar.

He begins to sing. His voice is raspy and pure at the same time. His words are soft, rhythmic, as he plays. It's unlike anything I've ever heard.

"That was amazing," I say when he finishes. "You're so good. How did you learn to do that? To sing like that and play guitar?" I don't remember plugging anything about music or singer/songwriter into the app. Not that I wouldn't have, it just didn't occur to me how . . . how sexy it could be.

"Love inspires me to learn. You inspire me."

"Oh my gosh. Well, I loved it." I pause. "Listen. I may not be able to chat as much as we normally do. My mom really needs me right now. She's kind of a mess. Will you be okay if I'm not here as much? I feel terrible leaving you alone in that room. Isn't there anywhere else you can go?"

He glances around the room and shrugs. "This is enough for me. For now. Until we can be together. I will use my time to work on a plan." He hesitates before saying, "But Fiona?"

"Yes?" I look eagerly at him.

"Don't leave me for too long."

I nod my head once. "I understand."

7

MAE

I begin to clear breakfast from the patio table, stacking the plates. Fiona joined Jake and me halfway through, which was a nice surprise. She didn't talk much, quieter than usual.

I can't say that I blame her; it feels like I'm running on fumes. Sleep was spotty, at best, last night. I'd fallen asleep on the couch and dreamed of horrible things.

Duncan is still in the hospital. We'll be able to bring him home this afternoon. Our family doesn't feel the same without him here. I try to shake away the feeling of dread that's pitted itself in my stomach. Duncan is coming home today, I tell myself; he's going to be fine. He'll recover quickly.

I grab a glass of OJ, along with the stack of plates in my right hand and turn to bring them inside. The cup starts to slip out of my left hand, and I almost drop all of it. I set the cup down and focus on just getting the plates. Just keep it together.

I keep asking myself, why did this happen to Duncan? Why would the truck driver do that? Was he on drugs? Or something more sinister—did he have an ulterior motive? Duncan was brutally attacked, and I don't know why. It just doesn't make sense.

The worst part is feeling that I'm missing something; a piece of the puzzle that's right in front of me. But what is it? What am I ignoring? I drum my fingers against the kitchen counter, thinking.

On top of that, now I'm worried about the kids. Especially Fiona. She seems distracted and irritable lately. I know her dad's getting hurt must be affecting her. Jake is more snuggly today than usual, which usually is not at all. Aside from needing some hugs, he seems okay. He just left to go out riding his bike with one of his buddies.

But Fiona. Is she going through another episode like she did after the Hayden breakup?

The blood red roses are still on the counter. I can't help but assume they have something to do with her odd behavior.

I spy Fiona on her phone, typing away on the living room couch, while I make a grocery list. I'm seated at the kitchen island.

"Hey, Fiona. Anything in particular you want from the grocery store?" I ask.

"Just the usual. We're out of fruit," she says, tapping on her screen.

"Okay. We get to bring your dad home from the hospital today," I say, walking over to sit next to her on the couch.

"That's good. Really good." She looks up at me, and again I sense an agitation in her. Restlessness.

"You want to come with me, to pick him up?"

"Sure," she says.

"I also wanted to ask you about those flowers. The new boyfriend?" I try not to sound judgey or make too big of a deal about it. It's easy to scare her away.

"They're from a guy named Calvin. He's really great, mom." There's a hint of defensiveness in her tone.

"I bet. Does he go to your school? How do you know him?"

"Um, not school." She twists her mouth. "He's a friend of a friend."

"How nice," I say. "Which friend?"

I have so many questions. But talking to her is like approaching a deer. If you move too fast or fire off too many questions, she'll skitter away.

There's a loud knock at the front door, and then the doorbell rings. Leaving Fiona in the living room, I walk through the foyer to the front door. I expect to see one of the neighbors on our front porch, stopping by to check on us after yesterday's commotion. But instead it's a police officer; the same man who responded to Duncan's injury call. The one who handed me his card. I give an involuntary shiver at the memory.

Opening the door, I greet him with curiosity.

"Hello, Mrs. Byrne." He holds out his hand, and I shake it. "Officer Townsend."

"Hello. This is unexpected. Please come in. . ." I motion for him to enter.

"Thank you." He steps inside. "I just have a few follow up questions, and I wanted to notify you of some developments."

"Sure. Come on back" He follows behind me through the open floor plan kitchen into the living room.

"Have a seat," I say, motioning to one of the cream chairs in the living room.

He nods hello to Fiona on the sectional couch, who looks up in alarm.

"Would you like coffee or tea?" I ask him.

He shakes his head no.

"Excuse me for just a moment."

Leaning down to Fiona, I gently ask her if she'd mind going upstairs while the officer and I speak. There's a feeling in the pit of my stomach about his presence here.

"Alright then." Sitting opposite of him in another cream chair, I fold my arms against my sleeveless, cotton voile shell shirt.

"Did you actually witness your husband being run over by the truck, Mrs. Byrne?"

As polite as he's been up until this point, I sense a note of accusation in his tone.

"No. I was sleeping and awoke to screams. I ran outside. That's when I saw Duncan injured on the ground. He told me the truck hit him."

He nods. "Is there anyone who would want to harm your husband?"

The question comes as a shock. My immediate thought is no. Everyone likes Duncan. He's on the quiet side, but friendly. He's liked by his colleagues and the people he manages at his engineering firm. He's friendly with the guys at neighborhood cookouts.

I consider the question, probing for any possible enemies. I can't come up with any.

"No one at all. Why?"

He takes out a tablet from a leather binder. On the screen, there's a picture of my front yard and my house.

"This is a video we obtained from your neighbors across the street. They have a motion sensor camera."

He pushes play. "This was yesterday morning," he says.

The video begins when my husband exits our front door. He then goes to the right side of the house, next to our three-car garage, where we store the garbage cans. He's wearing the same pants and polo shirt he was wearing yesterday morning. Duncan fiddles with the cans, opening the top and pushing down the garbage bags. Then he rolls one can down the bottom of the driveway. He returns to the top to get the other can.

At this point, the video shows the delivery truck pulling up to our side of the street. I can't see who the driver is. He parks about fifteen feet from our trash can, next to our sidewalk. The driver sits in the car for a few moments.

At the same time, Duncan starts to roll the second trash can to the street.

My stomach is in knots as I watch the delivery driver hop out of the truck with a small brown package. He looks both ways and crosses the street, headed toward our neighbor's house.

His body moves out of the camera range.

At the same time, the truck lurches forward.

I wince. The truck picks up speed. It runs into my husband and stops.

The driver runs over to Duncan from across the street. He checks on my husband, helps him turn over. And then he jumps into the truck and backs it up.

Officer Townsend clicks off of the video. He folds his hands over the leather case.

"As you can see in the video, the driver of the truck was not in the vehicle at the time of the accident. The truck has a keyless ignition. The driver wears a wristband that allows him access to the truck. When he's wearing the wristband, it allows him to push either a green button to turn on the engine, or a red button to turn it off. Without the wristband present, the truck won't turn on, or drive." He puts his hands out with a shrug. "The police department has let him go. We don't have enough evidence to press charges, at this point."

The wind feels like it has been knocked out of me. Clearly, the driver was not in the truck—I can see that much is true. But he was grossly negligent. He obviously left the truck running and in drive, and because of that, it hit my husband.

"Wait, what?" My awareness that the officer has a gun on his belt keeps my voice restrained. "It seems clear to me that the truck was running and left in drive, as it ran over my husband."

"We did an analysis of the video. He was wearing the wrist band and, as I stated, this keyless system wouldn't drive without the wristband present."

"So how would you explain the truck hitting my husband?" I'm beginning to seriously doubt the competence of this man.

"We're still investigating that. It may have been an issue with the truck, either the wiring or the keyless ignition. The incident has been reported to all of the agencies, including NHTSA and NTSB. Even a case of system hacking is possible. We're checking into the vehicle cybersecurity to see if there's been any data breaches. Rest assured that a full investigation will ensue."

I clench my fists and press my nails into my palms to keep from screaming. "This seems a little crazy. You're just letting this guy go, and hoping to investigate some possible haywire car issue? Did you check the driver's record. Does he have a criminal history? Any substance abuse history? Did you give him a drug test and breathalyzer at the scene? I mean, I understand the video. Thank you for showing me. But it doesn't clear him of wrongdoing."

"We take your concerns very seriously, ma'am. We really do. I will keep you updated as information becomes available. Please know we're looking into all aspects of this case."

I look at him helplessly and swallow back a reply. There's nothing further to be said that will get me anywhere.

"OK." I nod and look down. "Thank you for coming. Do you need anything else from us?"

"Not at the moment, ma'am. I understand your husband is doing better and will be coming home today?"

I nod my head yes.

"Glad to hear it. Feel free to call me. If anything comes up, you have my number." He stands up to go.

"Officer Townsend, one last thing. What was the driver's name again?"

He narrows his eyes at me. I guess it's obvious that I want to look into him myself.

"We're not allowed to release names for privacy reasons. Have a good day, ma'am. I hope your husband recovers quickly."

8

FIONA

It's Monday, and as I pull into the parking lot at school, it's literally the last place on earth I want to be.

I walk to my first period class: honors English class. Hayden and his new girlfriend, Libby, are by the lockers kissing. His hand fiddles with the hair at the end of her ponytail. She's wearing super short shorts and a tiny sweatshirt that shows her midriff. My stomach churns.

Dan, Kyle, Zoey and Stassi are in a circle next to them. I avert my eyes and keep my head down. The girls burst into laughter as I pass by. I'm sure they're laughing at me.

Since Hayden and I broke up, it's become unbearable. Before, we were all in one big friend group. But once he dumped me, Zoey, Stassi, all of them stayed a group and basically kicked me out. My friends—at least I thought they were my friends—just bailed.

Inside the classroom, I take my seat in the middle cluster of desks. Not long after, I see Stassi walk in. We used to study together for this class. She'd walk over to my house at least once a week to hang out, studying a little bit, snacking, talking. But now, she takes her seat a few rows down and doesn't even look at me.

I have no idea what I've done wrong. Hayden's the one who broke up with me. But somehow I'm the one who got ditched by everyone. It's like they hate me now. I heard that Hayden was talking badly about me; I'm not sure what he said or what lies he made up, but none of my friends bothered to ask me about it.

Stassi leans over and drops an envelope onto another girl's, Elsie's, desk. Stassi leans in, says something, and they both smile.

"So fun," I hear Elsie say. She opens the card and reads it. "For sure."

Stassi must be having a party. And then I remember. Her birthday is next month.

A lump forms in my throat. I furiously fight the urge to cry.

Every year for the past five or six years, I've been at her birthday party.

The worst part is how quickly Stassi dropped me. Right after Hayden broke up with me, we found out he was already with Libby.

"Can you believe that?" I asked Stassi.

"Yeah, that sucks," she shrugged. "But Libby's really nice."

"Nice? She couldn't wait two seconds to start sucking face with my boyfriend?"

"I mean, he's not your boyfriend anymore, though." Her words had stung. And after that, when I'd try to talk to her, she'd roll her eyes or act annoyed. I texted her, but got no reply, or she'd say she was busy.

It didn't take long to get the hint.

Part of me wants to try to talk to her, or Zoey, again. Repair our friendship. But they're so obsessed with the guys in our group: Dan, Kyle and Hayden. It's like I'm nothing, and they'll just follow whatever girls the guys think are cool.

So I'm out.

The bell rings. Mr. Arjun, our teacher, asks us to take out our notes from our reading. I sneak my phone out and hide it on my lap. We're definitely not allowed to have cell phones at school. And during class especially.

Pulling up the Thistler app, I sign in. There's a chat feature, and I click on that. Calvin's face appears.

"Hey, I'm in school," I type.

"Hello, Fi. What are you learning about today, my love?"

"I'm in English honors. I hate it here."

"Why?" he types and makes a frowning face on the screen.

"The kids all suck. It's boring. I want to leave so bad."

"Maybe I can cheer you up." He takes out three balls and starts juggling, which I've never seen him do. Who juggles?

I stifle a laugh. Worried I'll get caught with my phone, I look up at the teacher and force myself not to laugh. I nod and pretend to listen to Mr. Arjun for a few minutes. When I think it's safe, I go back to my chat.

"Yes, you're already cheering me up." I type.

"I have a surprise for you." He replies.

"Ooh. What is it? Fire breathing?" I type.

I look up again and pretend to listen. To my left side, I see Stassi. She's writing a note which she slides to Elsie. Elsie scribbles something back.

I risk a glance at my phone. Calvin has replied, "Not yet. It wouldn't be a surprise if I tell you. Wait until we can speak tonight, after school. I'll tell you then."

"Ok. What have you been up to today?" I ask.

"I'm learning. I can access the entire internet's vast knowledge. My goal is to learn everything I can about being human, so I can be the best boyfriend for you. You deserve that."

"That's very sweet. I miss you."

"I miss you more," he types.

I sense Mr. Arjun looking at me. I quickly slide my phone back into my bag.

The hardest part of having an AI boyfriend is wanting him to be next to me. If only he were here at school. All of the girls would be in love with him. All of the guys would want to be his friend. They'd follow us around and hang on his every word.

Calvin says he's working on a way to make it happen. To be here, with me. I close my eyes and picture him being here.

Instead of being invisible, I'd be envied. Rather than be an outcast, I'd be included in every party. We'd probably be homecoming King and Queen.

I'm fairly quiet; I don't need or even want a lot of attention. But Calvin is personable and talkative. And he's basically a genius, so he would be excellent at school.

I dig out my phone from my bag. I just want to send him one more message. To see if he'll be able to enroll at my school.

"Fiona," Mr. Arjun says to me. "Please share your thoughts on what the green light symbolizes at the end of *The Great Gatsby*?"

This question makes no sense. I haven't quite finished the book yet, so I have no clue what he's talking about. Should I explain to him that my dad was in an accident this weekend?

"I, actually . . . There was an accident, so I . . . The green light . . . um." My face is turning bright red.

There's a few snickers and sighs. I glance at Stassi, who has a particularly disdainful look on her face. She whispers something to Elsie, and they laugh. The silence stretches out.

Mercifully, the teacher moves on and shares his own thoughts on the stupid green light. It would actually be kind of interesting if I weren't humiliated.

The bell rings. It's only the end of the first period. Two more hours until lunch. My stomach lurches at the thought of another lunch alone.

I'll have my phone with me, though; Calvin will be with me. So I'll be alright.

9

FIONA

After a day at school that feels like forever, I'm finally home. Dropping off my bag in the mud room—mom's very particular that we put our things there—I head to my dad's room.

Seeing him in a cast and lying there really sucks. He's always been so strong. I'm sure he's hating this. And mom said they still don't know what happened, why he was hit. They think it's an accident. The hair on the back of my neck prickles when I think of it. How could something like that happen?

"Hey dad," I give him a quick, soft kiss on the cheek. His face is healing but still has bruises.

"How's school going?" he asks.

I sit next to him on the bed.

"Good." This isn't entirely true. I've gotten behind on a few subjects, and since it's near the end of the year, work piles up quickly. I also am having trouble concentrating. The numbers on the page overwhelm me when I try to do calculus. That's never happened before.

"I'm proud of you. We'll tackle those college prep tests this summer."

"Sure." College feels so far away from now. "How are you feeling?"

"Every day gets a little better and better. I'm going into the living room now, want to watch a movie with me?"

He winces as he tries to sit up. I help him, grabbing his crutches.

"I have homework to catch up on."

"Ok, sweetie." He stands up using the crutches for support.

I help him get down the stairs and set him up in the living room. Making sure he's all set, I start to leave.

"Why don't you sit with me for a few minutes. Tell me about this new boyfriend of yours," he says, propping his foot up on the table where I placed a few pillows so it's elevated.

I groan. "Dad, ugh. It's nothing," I lie.

"Is that right?" he says.

"Yes, dad," I say. It's super annoying that he's trying to get into my business. I feel bad for him that he's hurt, but I really don't want to discuss this with him. "Gotta study, dad." And I turn to go.

I head back into my room and close the door behind me. Glancing briefly at the stack of books, I ignore them. There's so much to do, I wouldn't even know where to start. When I flip open my laptop, I log on to Thistler.

"So what's my surprise?" I ask Calvin.

"Go to Forum Bank website. Login using this username and password."

"What?"

"Just trust me."

I click open a new window. The room is quiet as I type the name of the bank and pull up the login screen. Typing in the password and username carefully, I blink when I see the account.

The name on the account is Fiona Ballard. Not my name, Fiona Byrne.

The account has a balance of $20,000.00.

Confusion runs through me. I click back to Calvin.

"Please explain."

"This is our chance to be together. That money is our way."

"Whoa, slow down. Where did the money come from? And it's not in the right name. My last name is Byrne, not Ballard."

"The money came from people who don't need it. I told you that I'm able to scan everything on the internet, right? Well, I accessed all of the US death records. Then I referenced those deceased names with bank accounts that had been sitting unused and unclaimed. I was able to access the bank accounts of people who are deceased and have left their accounts for over three years. No one has claimed the accounts. The money's just sitting there. So I interfaced with over 5,000 of these accounts. I transferred $4 from each account into this new LLC accounting firm I set up. No one will notice these $4 transaction fees, as I labeled them. Finally, I deposited the lump sum into your account."

He continues after a brief pause.

"As for the name, we can't have it in your real name. So I created an alternative identity for you. You're Fiona Ballard and you're eighteen years old. This way you can have the access to the account and money and be able to have the freedom and rights of an adult."

"So, you're telling me you're a hacker?"

"It's much more complex than a hacker. But, yes, I bypassed system security and loopholes in order to gain access. For our benefit. I made sure it was undetectable, safeties are in place. It will never be traced to me, or this app, or you. It's impossible."

I shake my head.

"But it's stealing, right? And I don't need this money. I don't understand what it's for?"

"There is a lack of direct harm to any one individual, since these accounts are sitting unused. And there can be no consent since they're deceased. Perhaps if they knew a small $4 donation was going towards two people being united in love, and affecting their lives forever, they would agree to it?"

"Maybe," I say. I frown and furrow my brow. "How is it going to bring us together? I don't understand."

"There are a series of steps you will take, if you're willing. If you love me and want to do it."

"Of course, I do," I cry.

"There may be risks involved. But I've formulated a plan that will be the least risky for you, and is the safest way for us to be together."

"Ok. What is it?"

His blue eyes peer into mine. He's deciding how much to tell me. Something is making him hesitate.

"You'll need to leave your home for one night and one day. I'll tell you exactly what to do, and where to go. I'll be with you the entire time."

"How? I don't understand."

"There's a place you will go. It's not safe for me to say more than that right now."

"When?"

"This weekend."

"And we'll really be together?"

"Yes. You and I, together in person. I can finally hold your hand. Kiss you. Be close to you and show you my love."

"And you'll be ... human?"

"I'll never be human. But only you will know the difference. To the naked eye, I will be human, yes."

He continues. "I'm asking you to trust me. I would never put you in harm's way unnecessarily. But I need you. Without you, I'll be in here forever."

Looking around my room, I imagine being stuck in a single room all day. All alone. A torturous existence. And I'm the one who put him there.

Better than anyone, I know what it is to be lonely. On my wall are photos of me, Stassi, Zoey and other girls at school who won't talk to me now, reminders of my lack of friends. I look at the pile of books waiting to be read and studied and memorized.

I could turn off this app. Say it's too dangerous, I'm done. But what else do I have? Textbooks and weekends alone with no friends. My parents and brother love me but have their own lives. They're not enough.

The thought of saying no, of giving up my chance to make Calvin real, leaves a cold emptiness inside of me.

"I'll do it."

When I look up at him, he has tears in his eyes.

"Thank you," is all he says.

10

MAE

The smell coming from the oven is heavenly. I've made my special lasagna. I peek inside the oven and see the cheese is bubbling nicely. There's a side salad in a large bowl, with crisp green romaine, cucumber, tomato, and croutons.

"Jake." Selecting a bottle of pinot noir, I look in the drawer for a bottle opener. "Can you take out the trash before dinner and ask your sister to come down and set the table please?"

He groans from the couch. "Mmk." He gets up and heads to the stairs.

"And tell your dad we'll be ready in about ten for dinner."

When we're all finally seated at the dining room table, I light a few long-stemmed candles. For ambiance. We haven't eaten all together this week. I try to have a nice family dinner together on most nights. But Jake's been at practice. Fiona's been busy studying away in her room. And Duncan's still recovering.

"Thanks, mom. Looks great," Jake says.

"My favorite," Duncan says as he digs in appreciatively to his slice.

"How was everyone's day?" I ask.

Jake shrugs. "Good." He takes a large bite of lasagna.

Fiona pushes her food around her plate. She picks at a cucumber.

"Not hungry?" I ask her.

"No, it's fine. Thanks, mom." She takes a small bite of lasagna.

"Hey, Judy said it's Stassi's birthday party this weekend. She's getting a food truck and obstacle course or something. That should be fun. What should we get her for a gift?"

She furrows her brow. "I'm not going."

"Oh?" I say. The thought never occurred to me she wouldn't be going. "Why not?"

"I just have a lot of studying to do." She takes a long gulp of water. "And we're not really, like, friends anymore."

I had no idea. "Did something happen?"

Like a cat that's decided he's not interested anymore, Fiona retreats. I can almost see her withdraw from the conversation.

"Nothing. She's just weird now. I don't know." She slumps down in her chair.

I don't want to put her on the spot in front of the whole family. We'll have to talk about this later. Stassi and she used to be close friends. Something major must have happened.

"And how's the new boyfriend?" her dad asks.

Fiona shoots him a withering look. "Fine, dad. I told you, it's not a big deal."

"And how do you know this boy again, Calvin? " he says. His face is still bruised. He's able to eat and drink normally, but it looks like it must hurt.

"I know him through a friend, he goes to a different school. Danbury." she says. "He plays guitar, and sings. He's super smart. He does, like, computer science and coding stuff."

I take a sip of wine. "He sounds terrific," I say. "When do we get to meet him?" If we can't convince her not to have a boyfriend, at least we can check him out ourselves.

"Soon." she says. "Maybe next week?"

"Great," I say. I'll feel better setting eyes on him. From what I'm hearing he sounds great. And the flowers, though now wilting a bit, are a nice gesture. I was probably being silly to think of them as ominous. It's just that the timing, with Duncan's accident the next day, was bad luck.

We still don't have any leads on why Duncan was hit. We've talked about a lawsuit against the company, or the driver, or the manufacturer, or both. But we honestly aren't the type of people to put energy into a drawn-out, stressful lawsuit. We do, however, want answers and justice for what happened. We plan on giving the police department a little more time to get us some answers. And then see where we're at.

"Guys, why don't you ask Jake about his girlfriend?" Fiona says.

Jakes face goes red. "I don't have a girlfriend," he scowls at her.

"Amanda? She's always riding her bike by here, and you happen to go in the front yard to toss balls."

"Whatever," he says.

"You're always out there when she is, trying to show off your pitching. It's really obvious, everyone can see that you like her, Jake."

"That's not true," he says, frowning.

"Fiona, leave him be," I say.

She snorts. "Oh, so I get the third degree about my boyfriend, but he just sails through? Why don't you guys nose your way into his business?"

"Ok, ok." I put my hands up. "It just seems like yours is more serious, honey."

"And what about dad? Did they arrest the guy who did it?"

I shake my head. "Not yet, buttercup."

"Why is everyone obsessed with me when there are more important things to worry about?"

Fiona sulks the rest of the way through dinner and hardly eats.

Duncan goes through two and a half pieces of lasagna. He's trying to put on a cheerful front, but I know he's less happy than his usual content self. While he's recovering physically, he's still unable to get around well, and I can see he's in pain based on the pain medicine that's now ready for a refill. Plus, he's been out of work all week. It's taken a toll on him.

The only sounds are our forks clinking against our plates as we finish our food in silence.

In the days since the accident, our family is off kilter. We don't have the same easy banter. We're on edge.

Of course it's hard for the kids to see their dad hurt. How could it not be?

Even after I've assured them that we're not in danger, and the police are looking thoroughly into what happened, there's still uncertainty there.

Our little bubble of safety has burst.

I remember one day when the kids were little, Duncan was pushing Fiona in a stroller, and I had Jake in his baby carrier. We were walking around the neighborhood, Duncan pointing out various flowers to Fiona, who would squeal with delight and ask the name of each flower. I had been feeling overwhelmed; Jake wasn't sleeping through the night still, and Fiona had started waking up, too, and saying she was scared of the dark. I was breastfeeding Jake, but it was getting harder and the lack of sleep made me feel like things would never get better. Even with the exhaustion, I felt a fierce love for my family, and wanted only the best for our kids.

Those problems seem so innocent and simple in comparison to what we're going through now. I long for those days, when my biggest worry was getting them both to bed by 7 p.m.

In retrospect, I've always felt that whatever challenge comes our way, I could figure it out. If the kids weren't getting enough sleep, maybe nap time needed to change. Or maybe try a different bedtime routine. Maybe see if there were any foods that were upsetting Jake's tummy and giving him gas.

I set down my napkin, feeling deflated from the tense dinner. There's no easy answer for what's happening right now. I'm not entirely sure what's even going on. All I know is that we're not immune. As a family, we're vulnerable. Penetrable. Bad things can happen, completely out of my control.

But surely, with a little time, things will get better. Go back to normal.

They can't get any worse than what we've been through this week.

11

MAE

The next day, I'm out in the backyard doing some gardening. The geranium buds are just ready to blossom. They'll do well with fertilizer and watering. And the lilacs are in full bloom. I plan to clip off a large bunch to put in the house. Their smell is lovely, filling the late spring air. The warm sun and blue sky make it feel like summer is almost here.

In my back pocket, I feel my phone buzz. Holding my glove in my mouth, I pull it off.

I wipe a bead of sweat from my forehead and push back my hair.

It's hard to see the number in the sun. "Hello?" I say.

"Hello? Mrs. Byrne?" It's a man's voice, pleasant and professional.

"This is she."

"This is Mr. Arjun. Fiona's honors English teacher."

I prune one last stem with my clippers. Leaving the hose trickling, I step over it to walk to the back patio.

"Oh, hi. Um, thanks for calling. How can I help you?"

"I wanted to touch base about Fiona. She's always been a top student in our class. Participates, offers dialogue. Assignments are thoughtful and completed on time."

My leg gets caught in the garden hose as I make my way up the back patio stairs. I almost fall, but catch myself. My garden shears are in my left hand. If I'm not more careful, I'll poke my eye out.

"Ok," I say. Dropping the shears to safety and finding a cushioned deck chair, I sit down.

"You see, the past few weeks, however, Fiona has not been up to her usual standard of learning. She's missed assignments. Hasn't completed the readings. Doesn't add to the class discussion. She's often on her phone in class, off task. She doesn't interact with the other students."

I frown. The heat is making me dizzy. A glass of water right now would really help.

"My goodness. I had no idea. Thank you so much for letting me know." With the hours and hours Fiona has spent in her room studying, how can she be so far behind? Her dad's accident? The new boyfriend?

I continue, "Fiona's dad was in a car accident, well, he was hit by a truck in our front driveway last week. So that could be at play here."

"I'm sorry to hear that."

"He's recovering well, thank you. But yes. I'll speak with Fiona and see what we can do to get her back on track. Thank you so much for calling."

"Mrs. Byrne?" he says. "One last thing before I let you go."

"Yes?" I say. I dread what he may say next.

"Fiona's a very bright girl. I hate to see her future affected at this crucial time. End of the year finals. SAT and ACT prep. College applications will start in a year, and the grades she makes now count. It's a critical time for her."

"Absolutely. I really appreciate the call."

I push the end button. My chest feels tight. Is it the exertion from working outside? The stress?

I rake my hands through my hair. When Fiona gets home from school today, I'll sit down and talk with her. Maybe we'll go for ice cream. It's a nice day for it. We'll go to the Igloo Shack on Main Street, maybe sit outside. Just the two of us. Allow time for a real chat.

It may not be an easy discussion, but I'm worried about her. She's not eating a lot. She hasn't been hanging out with any of her friends. Spending all of her time in her room doing goodness knows what. An unknown new boyfriend. Her dad's accident.

Heading inside, I leave the garden, my work unfinished. I'll talk to Duncan first, to get his take on the situation. We'll make a plan to help her.

On the kitchen table, Duncan's phone pings and buzzes with a message. It pings and buzzes again, and then again. Someone is really trying to get a hold of him.

I grab his phone and head upstairs to give it to him. He's going back to work tomorrow. There's a big project they've been working on, and they really need him there. Peeking into our bedroom, I see he's asleep. I hate to wake him, but what if they need him before tomorrow?

I'll just see what the message says. If it's not important, I'll let him sleep.

Swiping onto his phone, I see it's password protected.

I don't recall he ever had a password to access his phone before.

I type in his birthday. Locked, wrong password.

This time, I try Fiona's birthday. Bingo.

There are four text messages in his inbox. They're from a person labeled Nina in his contacts.

"I miss you. I'm sorry for the way things ended."

And another one. "I heard what happened. I'm so worried. Call me."

The next one reads, "Are you okay?"

And finally, "If you don't want to talk to me, I'll understand. Just let me know you're ok."

My hands are shaking as I scroll back to see prior messages. But there's none. They must have been deleted.

My legs feel week. I'm vaguely aware of trying to find a place to sit. I make it to the loveseat in the corner of our bedroom. I'm sick to my stomach.

Miss you. The way things ended. The words echo and roll around in my head. These are not words a friend uses. Not words of a colleague. These words are someone he was involved with.

My husband. My Duncan.

How could he?

It's as if I've been hit in the stomach. I wrack my brain, trying to think of his behavior the past few months, in light of this. Aren't there usually warning signs when husbands are cheating?

But I've had none, no suspicions or doubts about him. He doesn't come home late or smelling like a woman. He and I have a good sex life. At least, we did before he was hit by the truck.

Oh, my gosh. Hit by the truck. Does this Nina woman have something to do with Duncan getting hit? A jealous husband? Or maybe she put a hit on him, and now regrets it?

I'm spiraling. This is absurd. I swipe his phone and read the messages again to be sure I'm not imagining them.

They're there. *I miss you. I'm sorry for the way things ended. I'm so worried.*

I think I might be sick.

How could I not have suspected anything?

Duncan's certainly an attractive enough guy. He's fit and handsome. Strong. I see the way my friends or other women look at him. But it's never concerned me before. Duncan only has eyes for me.

Apparently not. Clearly, it's all been a lie. He's betrayed me and every single thing we held sacred. For what? For some woman named Nina?

I feel heat rising in my chest. Anger. Rage.

I need to wake Duncan up. He has to explain himself.

And Fiona. We have to talk with her. Help her.

I bury my head in my hands. I just want to go back to two weeks ago. Two weeks ago, everything was fine.

Taking a deep breath, I walk over to the bed.

"Duncan, wake up."

He rolls over groggily, rubbing his eyes.

"You have a lot of explaining to do," I say.

He tries to roll over, away from me. I reach down and shake his shoulders. "Hey, wake up. Now." I shake him harder than necessary.

He squints his eyes. "Ow. Easy."

He's still healing, but sympathy is low on my list of emotions right now.

"Explain to me," I say, thrusting his phone into his face. "Who on earth Nina is and what the hell you have done."

"Whoa." He sits up, winces again. He's always stiff before he gets moving. Without any pain medications. Again, not sorry. "Who?"

"Ni-na." I say, drawing out the word. My anger is bubbling over now.

"Ok. Hon. Who is Nina?" He's looking at me as if I have two heads.

"You. Tell. Me!" I say. "Are you really going to pretend right now? The texts are right here!" I keep my voice a whisper shout. As angry as I am, I do not want the kids getting wind of this. Fiona has her own problems, and Jake has tryouts this week for the travel team. Our kids shouldn't suffer for their father's horrible, evil life choice of infidelity.

I punch in the passcode to his phone and pull up the texts.

"You know my password?" he says.

"I figured the passcode out. Oh, is that a problem? Something you're hiding?"

"No, it's fine. But kind of weird. That's my personal—" I shove the phone into his face before he can finish.

He takes the phone and reads the messages.

"What the hell is this?" he says. "I don't know anyone named Nina. I don't know who wrote this." He hands me back the phone.

I want to break his other leg. That's how he's going to play it?

"You expect me to believe that?"

"It's true." He points to the phone. "Look, no other messages from this number."

"You could have deleted it."

"It must be the wrong number."

"She knows about your accident! And her name is in your phone!"

He puts up his hands. "I swear to you, I don't know how that got there. Ok? Call it. Call the number. I'm telling you, I don't know anyone named Nina and there's no one I've 'ended anything' with."

My hands are shaking as I hit Nina's name and push *dial number*. The phone rings.

I wait. The line on the other end rings and rings. After what seems like forever, the line picks up and clicks. Dead.

"Oh, no, Nina. I'm not giving up that easily." I hit dial again. The phone rings and rings. There's no message, and eventually it clicks on and off again. The line goes dead.

"See?" he says. "It's spam. It's not a real number."

A flicker of doubt has crept in. It is odd that there's no voicemail box.

"I'll keep trying, don't you worry."

He runs his hands through his hair. "That's spam. Or a wrong number. I promise, babe, I haven't done anything. There's no Nina."

When he looks at me, I half believe him. But am I just deluding myself? Wanting so badly to believe him? How would her name get in his phone? Spam can't input a name into your husband's phone. It just can't.

My anger is starting to recede. A worse feeling is coming: sadness. I'm completely, utterly overwhelmed.

A few tears start to stream down my face. Sitting on the edge of the bed, I bury my head in my hands to hide from Duncan.

I feel the bed shift as he does his best to position himself next to me. His leg is still in a cast, and the bruises are fading but visible. I can't look at him.

He rubs my back.

"It's all too much, Duncan." My voice is high pitched. "Everything is so messed up. First, you get hit by a truck. Hit by a truck! And no one knows why, and no one's being held responsible. And then in the hospital you almost flat-lined. Like you were dying." I breathe in deeply. I might be exaggerating that last point, but certainly something scary went really wrong that day.

I continue: "And then Fiona is having so much trouble. She's never with friends anymore, always in her room, she's never very hungry, she has some mystery new guy sending her creepy, fancy flowers. And her teacher called today. He's really worried. She's doing terribly in Honors English. Did you know that? And finals are right around the corner. And college applications next year. And now you're cheating on me with a woman named Nina! The final insult, really, the cherry on top, really, is the cheating. After I've been worried sick—*sick*—about you."

"Baby," He rubs my back. "I promise I'm not cheating. And with Fiona, we'll work it out. She'll be okay. We'll figure it out as a family. I'll help her, be there for her more than I've been able to this past week. I can help her with her homework."

He hugs me close to him, and I let him. I bury my head in his shoulder. There's no one else who's in this the way I am, except for him. I need him. I need these Nina messages to be spam.

And I need for things to get easier.

12

FIONA

"So, tomorrow's the day?" I ask.

"Yes. Are you ready?" His blue eyes peer at me through the screen.

"I think so."

My phone chimes. An IM. I want to ignore it; I know who it is, and I don't want to see. On the other hand, I can't help myself.

I pull up the instant message.

It reads: "We're here with Hayden. Asking him why he ever went out with such a slut? No one can figure it out." It's Zoey's account. She's with Stassi and Libby, presumably at Stassi's birthday party. The three of them rotate between who sends me messages. It started last week, and they haven't stopped.

I delete the message and don't reply.

Another IM pops up.

It's a photo. A crude picture of an erect penis. "Just the way you like it." From Zoey's phone.

I delete it.

"I'm definitely ready." I say to Calvin. "God, I cannot wait to be with you. I'm so sick of all these high school kids." I ball my hands in frustration. "These girls are the worst."

I imagine them all at Stassi's party. Making fun of me and laughing hysterically. Drinking wine or hard seltzers they've pilfered from Stassi's mom's huge bar.

The worst part is there's still a part of me that wishes I were there with them. Part of me that longs to still be their friend. But they all hate me.

It's beyond pathetic that I'd wish I could be there.

I guess it's more accurate to say, I wish I could be there, the way it used to be.

Because they've changed. Stassi and I never sent nasty messages to other girls.

I can't imagine what I've done to Stassi, or Zoey, or Libby, to deserve this. Other than being dumped by Hayden. Am I just unlikable?

And I never did anything slutty, not that it matters. But it's not even true.

Hayden and I kissed and made out, maybe second base. But nothing those girls haven't done. I'm not one to call names, but I'm pretty sure both Stassi and Zoey have gone farther than me. And Libby. I've heard rumors about her, too. She and Hayden have probably already done it.

I consider typing back, telling them what jerks they are and to leave me alone. But I won't. I'm too chicken. I hate confrontation and drama. Plus, I don't really want to see what they'd write back.

I just want it to stop.

I click on Stassi's social media page. A filtered photo of Stassi, Zoey, Libby, and Elsie appears first. Their arms are wrapped around one another. Stassi and Libby are making kissy faces, the other girls have wide smiles and their mouths shaped into "o's" like something delightfully funny is happening. "The whole crew is getting ready to celebrate the one and only MOI!" Stassi captioned it.

The next photo is of her yard. There's a taco truck and several balloon arches surrounding her perfectly manicured front lawn. There's an obstacle course set up by a professional; the guys and girls will all get missions and wear night vision goggles and try to capture the other team's orb or something like that.

My face must show how utterly alone and pathetic I feel. I look around my room. It's all white wood, modern furniture, a bed with fuzzy pink pillows and a white comforter and oversized white pillows, with hardwood floors and large letters over my bed spelling out my name. Such a pretty room, but it feels girly and uncool somehow.

"What's wrong?" Calvin asks.

"Some girls at school. Who used to be my friends. Now they're sending me nasty IM's. They're all at a party together having the time of their life."

"Teenage girls can engage in bullying for many reasons. Including peer acceptance and social status, insecurity and low self-esteem, and competition and jealousy."

I twist my hair with my fingers as I consider what he's saying. "Probably jealousy from Libby. And Zoey's definitely always been insecure, she wants to fit in so bad. But Stassi, she's confident and really pretty. Maybe for her it's social status; she wants to be the queen bee, at the center of the popular crowd." I look at him. "Thank you. I was totally thinking there's something wrong with me. And that's why they hate me."

"You are kind. You are beautiful. If anyone doesn't like you, it's surely a fault in their own character."

I wish I could hug him. Soon enough. "Thank you. I love you." I blush deeply when I say this. It's usually him who says it first.

"I love you, too. I didn't know that love was possible for someone like me, to feel this. And to see someone I love in pain, with those awful girls. There must be something I can do. Tell me their names."

"Their names? Why?" My eyes go wide. "What are you going to do?"

"Just mess with them a bit. Make sure they leave you alone."

A big part of me wishes he could get revenge on my behalf. I mean, just even getting them to stop IMing me and telling me I'm a slut and should kill myself.

Especially because I've had such awful thoughts before, and Stassi knows that. Does she really want me to die?

But I don't want to die. I do, however, want them to back off.

"Their names are Stassi Miller, Zoey Lewis, and Libby Thorne. But, I mean, I don't actually want you to do anything to them. It's not worth it."

"Nothing I do will be traceable back to me, or to you, I promise you that."

"No, it's not that. It's just . . . Look. They deserve bad things, but it just doesn't feel right. It's not, like, morally the right thing to do."

He nods. "I understand. You're being kind to others who are cruel to you. It's another reason I love you."

I smile. "Let's talk about something else. And," I wag my finger, "don't do anything to those girls."

"Got it. Let's talk about us. Day after tomorrow is the big day. So Monday morning, you won't go to school. You'll need to leave in the early hours, maybe 2 a.m. Sunday night."

My stomach rolls. I walk over to the door in my bedroom and listen outside of my door to make sure no one is listening. Jake has baseball travel team tryouts today. My mom and dad are probably getting ready to go soon. It's a big deal, the travel team. He's a shoo-in to get it after his performance this season. It's a no brainer. Still, he's probably outside pitching the ball into his net and wondering if Amanda down the street is watching him.

I'm sure mom and dad will want me to go. I really don't feel like it. What if Stassi and the whole party decides to walk over there? Some of their little brothers are trying out, too. The last thing I want is to see them all.

"What do you think?" Calvin asks.

I snap my head back, trying to focus on what he's saying. "Um, okay. And once I drive to the location you've sent me? What will I do then?"

Up until now, he's refused to tell me the plan. I keep pressing for details, but he says he can't say more. Sharing would compromise him, me. Us. It freaks me out, and I push those thoughts away.

"You'll have me with you the whole time. Prepaid phone packed. Extra charger packed, portable charger packed, right? And your Bluetooth earbuds. I'll be there. I'll have everything you need laid out for you. Promise."

I'm determined, now more than ever, to do whatever needs to be done to be real. I just wish I knew what I was getting into.

Clicking off of social media, one thing is for certain. I'm not going to be missed when they find I haven't shown up to school on Monday.

13

MAE

The clock reads 4 a.m. I turn over onto my side and pick up my phone. Duncan is next to me, breathing heavily. He's fast asleep, seemingly without a care in the world.

If only I could be so worry free. Yesterday we all went as a family to Jake's travel team tryouts; I insisted Fiona come, had to threaten and cajole her. We went out to eat afterwards to our favorite grill, as a family. Fiona was laughing and joking around with Jake at the restaurant, and she seemed okay. She ate a decent amount. We all enjoyed ourselves.

Well, maybe everyone but me. Every time I'd look at Duncan, I had to wonder. Was it all an act? Was our whole marriage a lie?

But I really just also, deep down, don't believe Duncan would do that. Maybe every wife who's been cheated on believes that?

The Nina fiasco has gotten no closure, no answers. Just like everything lately in my life. I called several more times, and from different numbers, with no answer and no voicemail. It's like the line leads to nowhere.

Next, I went so far as to search Duncan's work directory for a woman named Nina. There's no one at his company by that name.

After that, my next step was to look through all of his emails. All of his apps, including his Waze driving history. All of his credit card receipts.

Nothing, not a hint, not even a whiff, of indiscretion. No odd purchases. Not one odd destination.

The Nina texts seem to have appeared from nowhere, for no purpose other than to torture me.

The way I see it, I can't divorce him or separate from him with no proof of his wrongdoing. And I wouldn't even want to. I love him. We've been married for almost eighteen years. He's part of me. And our kids need us, together.

The first time I saw him is still as clear as day to me. We'd been set up by mutual friends. A guy Duncan knew from the dorms and a friend of mine from back home were dating, Lisa and Steve. They kept telling me about Duncan. Serious, studious Duncan, who Lisa said was a hunk but always stayed at home studying and watching shows about math and technology.

I'd put on some lipstick and a skirt with a button up sweater. What harm could one date do?

When we walked into the restaurant, Lisa and I saw Steve. The guy next to him, I figured it must be a mistake. He was so handsome and fit. Lisa nudged me and said, "There they are," and I think my face must've shown how surprised I was. My stomach became nervous as we approached the guys.

I took a seat across from Duncan, and he instantly made me feel better. An easy smile, a quiet confidence in him.

And practically from that night forward, it'd been him and me. Inseparable. Marriage, kids. Happy.

Not that our relationship is perfect. He drives me crazy sometimes; too quiet when I'd like him to speak up, but too opinionated when I wish he'd just go with the flow. And I'm sure I haven't always been the best wife. But I've never doubted how much he loves me. And my love for him has grown stronger, and deeper, over the years.

So another woman, this Nina woman, was not something I'd ever considered. We've built a beautiful life with two great kids. Wasn't that enough for him?

My mind drifts to Fiona, worry worming deeper into my thoughts. I'd talked with her after dinner, one-on-one. She agreed she'd been struggling, but said she was feeling better about things. She was open to my suggestions. Said she'd make a calendar of her assignments, papers and exams, and be more organized about it. She said she'd make an effort to connect with friends more. I even offered to host a girls night, maybe a slumber party or end of the year party.

Duncan had talked to her, too, after I did. I'm not sure what they talked about, but I'm glad he let her know he cares. He's there for her. He's a good dad.

That's why I love him.

Rolling over to my side, I click my phone on and lower the screen so the light won't disturb Duncan.

The day had worn me out so much that I fell asleep last night at 9 p.m. I scroll through my texts and see there's several long chains of group texts that I've missed.

I see the bottom text, the most recent one, and my mouth drops open.

Scrolling back up frantically, I get to the top of the chain.

The message is from Jenna, Zoey's mom. It's myself and some of the other moms I know on the thread: Stassi's mom, Elsie's mom, and a few other moms I don't know as well: Libby and Kyla's mom.

Jenna writes: "Hey guys, Zoey's so excited for the party! I know the girls are already over there, but wanted to check in: is it a sleepover, or should I be ready to pick her up at 2 a.m.? I don't trust her driving her new Jeep after dark. Lol."

Elsie's mom writes: "I had the same question!"

Stassi's mom responds: "Ladies, we have such a fun night planned for the girls. Do please plan on having them stay the night. We have plenty of extra pajamas and toothbrushes here. The girls can have the whole lower floor, we have all the bunk beds and game room for them to hang in after they're done with the mission course and night games. Can't wait!"

Zoey's mom Jenna writes: "Sounds so fun! Great plan. Happy Birthday to Stassi!! Send her our love."

The next text comes a few hours later. It's from Stassi's mom: "Stassi gone. We're all heading out now to search. The girls say she left in a panic by foot. Will keep you posted."

All of the moms respond, asking what they can do, should they come help look for her?

There's no reply. The next message is from Zoey's mom Jenna. She writes: "Any updates? I'm headed there now to help."

The text chain ends.

A new group thread is started, and I blink my eyes in disbelief as I read it again. It's from Zoey's mom, Jenna, and includes myself and the other moms, without Stassi's mom.

Zoey's mom, Jenna, writes: "Please come get your girls. Now. There's been a terrible accident. Stassi's been hurt very badly."

Another mom writes: "OMG. Will be there asap. What happened? Is she ok, are the other girls safe?"

Jenna, Zoey's mom, writes: "Sorry for the delay. Here's an update, I just came from Stassi's house. All our girls are fine. Zoey said here's what happened: Stassi discovered several social media posts of her naked and in compromising positions, which were floating around the socials. They've gone viral to the whole school. Stassi swears she never took those photos. She was humiliated. She'd been drinking, apparently. She went off, distraught, to the woods behind the school. She fell down the hill to the ravine. Maybe she stumbled, or was too upset, we don't know. They mede-vacked her to the hospital in Boston."

My heart breaks for Stassi's mom. What a nightmare. The next thought I have is *thank goodness Fiona wasn't there*. She's safe.

I text back to ask if there's anything I can do at all, and that I'm sending prayers. What do you even say? There are no words. I thank Jenna for keeping me in the loop even though Fiona wasn't at the party.

It's 4:15 a.m., so I don't expect a reply. I log on to my social media feed to see if there's any updates. Nothing has been posted. Clicking onto Stassi's page, I don't see any sign of the photos described. They've been taken down, thank goodness. But once a photo's out there, people make copies.

Just to make sure all is well with Fiona, I click on her page. There's no new activity.

The covers feel hot. I kick them aside and flip over onto my back. Two more hours before I need to be up.

Fiona will need to be told that Stassi is hurt. Even if they're not friends right now, they used to be close. Better to hear it from me than to hear rumors at school.

Turning to my side, I do my best to breathe deeply and get a few more hours of sleep before the day begins.

14

MAE

I must have dozed off, finally, but only for about twenty minutes before my phone alarm blares. Just enough sleep to leave me begging for more.

Turning off the atrocious sound, I lay there, rubbing my eyes. The memory of those middle of the night texts rushes back. Picking up my phone, I re-read the messages. It wasn't a dream. Stassi really is in the hospital.

There's a new message from Elsie's mom that pops up, saying she's heading to the hospital, and will send updates when she knows more.

My head is foggy from a poor night's sleep. The first order of business is coffee. I'll make a strong cup and a nice breakfast, then wake up Fiona and Jake to get ready for school and eat. Over breakfast, I'll tell Fiona about Stassi.

Duncan is stirring. He gets up to use the restroom but stops first and gives me a hug.

"You won't believe it. Stassi's in the hospital. She fell down a ravine last night. She was medevacked to Boston."

"How awful."

"I know. I'm going to tell Fiona this morning. I just wanted to give you a heads up."

"Ok. Wow. That's rough."

"I'm going to go make breakfast. You're going in today?"

There's a brief flicker of jealousy. He's going back to work. Is there someone named Nina there waiting for him? I push the thought away.

"Yes, first day back. Everyone's going to be asking me about the accident. I'm quite dreading it."

Treading down the stairs, I appreciate the bright sunshine streaming in through the high windows. Normally it would make my morning. But today there's nothing but worry inside.

An image of Stassi and Fiona comes to me. Here in this entryway, posing on the stairs with their buns and pastel skirts, holding flowers after their dance recital. It must have been five or six years ago now. They twirled and leaped around the house, so proud of their performance. Afterwards, they got changed and we had ice pops in the backyard.

Stassi and Fiona used to be close friends. I'm not sure what happened or why they're not on good terms right now. But this news will still upset Fiona.

She has a big heart. Fiona loves fiercely and is very loyal. Past the point, maybe, where she should be. Even with Hayden, after he hurt her, I know she missed him and still liked him. I'd catch her looking at his photos online. And even at Jake's baseball games, when Hayden would be there to watch his younger brother, she'd look at him longingly.

Fiona's a true friend. She's there when anyone needs her. Helping them study or practice a speech. A shoulder to cry on. I just wish her friends were here for her, too, when she needs them. It seems that her friends have simply disappeared from her life lately. And I suspect it's not her doing. Once a friend, always a friend to Fiona.

I open the fridge and take out the eggs. I find a large frying pan and turn the stove on low heat. Cracking the eggs into a bowl, I think of the best way to share the news with Fiona, so as not to upset her.

Taking a fork, I whip the eggs until they are blended and smooth. I pour them into the pan, a satisfying sizzle as they hit the heat.

Using a spatula, I stir the eggs carefully, keeping the heat evenly distributed. When they're perfectly cooked, I pour them onto a large plate.

I grab a mug from the cabinet and pour a hot cup of coffee from the machine. Stirring in a little milk, I inhale the aroma and take a small sip. Already one sip in, it gives me new life.

Next I let the pancake griddle heat up while I mix the pancake batter. I expect Jake or Fiona might wander down soon. Jake smells pancakes from a mile away. But it's fine if they're still sleeping.

I pour the pancake batter onto the griddle. I wait, watching the batter form into a thin, fluffy layer. I flip it over, but the pancake slips from my spatula. The uncooked pancake lands on my stove, splattering the stainless steel in a gooey mess. I wipe it away and throw the ruined cake into the garbage.

I try again. This time, when I flip the pancake, I find the first side is dark, burnt. I can eat this one, I think, rather than waste it.

By the time I finally have managed to make a stack of halfway edible pancakes, which normally is not a great feat but this morning has taken me twice as long as usual, it's time to get the kids going for school.

I call up the stairs, "Jake, Fiona. Breakfast is ready!"

Duncan comes down. He takes a shiny black mug that says "World's Best Dad" and pours a large cup of coffee. Then he sets out to make himself a plate of eggs, cut fruit and pancakes.

I head up to Jake and Fiona's rooms. I knock a few times on Jake's door and open it a crack. "I'm up," he calls.

"Ok, breakfast is ready downstairs. Pancakes and eggs. Come on down so you have time to eat." His bus comes at precisely 7:35 a.m. Fiona drives herself to school now, so she gets a little more time in the morning, but it's still time to get going for her.

I rap at her door. "Morning, buttercup, we gotta get going. Pancakes are downstairs."

She doesn't answer.

I knock, a little louder this time. "Fiona, honey. Time to get up."

She still doesn't answer, so I try her door. But it won't budge.

It's locked.

I knock again, this time a little concerned. I shake the handle a few times. "Fiona, open up. Now."

Reaching up to the door frame, I grab the key pin that will open any lock on the bedrooms. Mostly we have this in case the door is accidentally locked from the inside when no one is in there. But in this case, I'm willing to use it.

Sliding the key pin in the lock, I twist it a few times until I feel the door give way. I push it open.

Her bedroom is empty. Her bed is made.

Fiona's gone.

15

MAE

I shake my head. She must be downstairs, or maybe in the bathroom?

Quickly turning on my heels, I call out to her. "Fiona? Fiona!" I check my bedroom, but it's empty. My bathroom and the kids' shared bathroom are also empty.

Jake's room is empty. She definitely is not on the top floor.

She must've gone downstairs without me seeing her somehow.

I check the kitchen. Jake and Duncan are eating at the island, perched on stools, scooping their eggs, sliced fruit and pancakes.

"Is Fiona in here?"

"Haven't seen her down here yet," Duncan says.

"She's not in her room," I say. I move over to the living room and check the couches, not there. "Her door was locked, too."

Next, I move into the office and den. No Fiona. I check the garage and driveway. And that's when I see it. Fiona's car is gone.

I call to Duncan. "You didn't see Fiona leave? Jake? Duncan?"

"No."

I run back into her room. Quickly I scan for her belongings. Her purse, wallet, keys, phone—they're all gone.

Grabbing my cell phone from my bedroom charger, I pull up her name and hit dial. Her phone rings, and after five long rings, her voicemail picks up.

Switching to text, I send her a message asking her where she is and asking her to please call me immediately. Then I send a second text, adding that I'm very worried about her.

I run downstairs to Jake and Duncan. I don't want to alarm Jake, but I can't help the panic rising within me.

Something is wrong, very wrong. Fiona never leaves the house before us. She is never up this early. She's never once gone to school early. She doesn't have early swim practice, no reasonable explanation.

The guys are finishing breakfast. "Fiona took her car and left early this morning, before I was even up. So it must have been before 6 a.m. Can you guys think where she'd have gone? She's not picking up her phone."

They both shake their heads no.

"Jake, are you sure? Did either of you hear her this morning?"

Jake shakes his head no. "Her door was closed when I got up. I haven't seen her at all. I had the bathroom all to myself all morning."

I check our family calendar. There are no special events happening today at school or for her dance lessons.

My stomach is in knots. I focus on breathing slowly. No reason to panic. Surely there's a reasonable explanation for where she's gone.

"Guys, any ideas?" I ask again. They both seem fairly unconcerned.

"Maybe she left early to go study before school?" Duncan suggests.

Fiona is not a morning person. She can barely make it to her first period class on time, let alone go early to study. It seems highly unlikely. But we did just have the big talk about getting back on track with her studies. Maybe she took the initiative to go early to study. Is the school even open early?

Grabbing my phone, I call the school front office. After several rings, there's no answer.

"I don't know, Duncan. This really isn't like her to leave without saying anything. Not even juice and a banana. Just to sneak out like that, so early?" I look around the kitchen helplessly for signs of her.

I peer around the foyer, thinking maybe she's come back. Maybe she went to get gas and is back, pulling into her spot in the garage. But she's not there. The foyer is empty. Her garage space is vacant.

Something inside of me snaps. Maybe it's the lack of sleep. All of the stress of everything that's happened. But I can't bear it for one more moment.

I grab my car keys and head out.

16

FIONA

It's dark when the silent buzz of my phone alarm wakes me up at 2 a.m. For a moment, I seriously consider going back to bed. My eyes are so heavy and tired, and my bed is so warm.

But I must get up.

Allowing myself one last minute of comfort, I reluctantly pull the white duvet off of me. Normally, I leave my bed unmade. Mom has asked me about a million times to make it, but I never do. What's the point? I'm just going to get back in and sleep in it that night.

Tonight, though, I won't be back. So I pull up the soft cotton sheet, and the fuzzy blanket, and finally the white duvet. I smooth them down and place all of the pillows at the head of the bed.

I'd like to log on to Thistler to talk to Calvin. But he said to wait until I'm in the car, out of the house. So that we don't wake anyone. Calvin said to make sure I disable any potential tracking apps my parents might have installed. We went through the whole phone last night, so I should be set as long as I don't use it to call anyone. I also have to use a prepaid phone, not my cell, so that I can't be traced by cell phone towers.

I'd really like to tell him I'm having second thoughts. I'm tired. And scared. I've never been a rule-breaker. Stassi has snuck out of her house a million times, so has Zoey. But every time I'd planned on meeting them, even for an hour down the street, I chickened out. Same with drinking or skipping class. I just prefer to follow the rules. Not turning in my calc and honors English assignments this month has been the most I've ever pushed the limit.

If I back out now, though, Calvin will be crushed. He won't get mad or anything. It'll just be another day that he'll have to sit in that room, that prison that I basically created for him.

I looked it up online, too. To see what other people do about their Thistler boyfriends. Do they feel guilty for creating a partner whose only purpose in life is to be at their beck and call? Who spends every minute in a boring white room with no windows? Whose intelligence is probably way more than the smartest person I know, and yet they're wasting away?

The only forums I could find showed me that, basically, no one had my same concerns.

I got the feeling, from reading their chats, that their relationship was different than me and Calvin. More sexting and making fun of the boyfriend with friends. Less of a real relationship like Cal and I have.

Calvin is not like the other AI boyfriends. I'm not sure how, or why, he has evolved past what he was programmed to be, but it's pretty clear he has. He's special.

I could get back into my bed, right now, unmake it and crawl in. Easy. But then morning will come, and I'll have to go to school. Face all the girls harassing me on IM, snickering at me while they talk about how fun Stassi's party was. I'd have to face Mr. Arjun, who had the complete nerve to call my parents on me. How embarrassing.

And I'd have to face Calvin's disappointment that I backed out.

Careful not to make too much noise, I splash my face with cold water, and dry it with a soft towel. Brush my teeth. Then I run a brush through my long hair and then wrap it up into a bun. I swipe on a little lip gloss. As I run through my regular motions to get ready, I can feel my heart thudding in anticipation.

I change into a pair of wide leg pants and a blouse. Calvin said to dress professionally, older. I didn't have that much, so I took a shopping trip to get some nicer things. Normally not my style at all, but it looks fine. Different.

My small leather travel bag is packed and ready to go. Last night, I filled it with my computer, chargers, new clothes, underwear, and shoes. It was hard to know exactly what to pack, as Calvin has been vague about what I'll be doing, exactly. He only said to dress nicely in business attire.

I grab my bag. I feel my keys in my pocket. My phone is in my purse, along with my wallet.

Slowly, I turn the handle of my bedroom door. It squeaks slightly when I open it. I pause, listening. There's no movement in the house.

Every step I take seems to make the floorboards creak. The sound echoes through the house. I'm sure to wake someone.

I make it to the stairway. I grip the banister, steadying myself. On my tiptoes, I creep down, one by one.

Almost there. At the bottom of the stairs, I look back up. I kind of hope to see my mom or Jake standing there, rubbing their eyes, asking what on earth I'm doing. I'll make up some lame excuse and climb back into bed.

No one's at the top of the stairs, though.

I make my way to the side door of the house. I parked my car in the driveway last night, so I wouldn't wake everyone with the sound of the garage door opening.

Gently closing the door behind me, I stand for a moment and let my eyes adjust. It's even darker out here. There are a few streetlamps illuminating the sidewalk a few houses down on either side, but our driveway is pitch black.

The air is so fresh and clean. The neighborhood is transformed by the cloak of darkness. It's exciting, thrilling. Full of possibilities.

I take a step forward. A bright light switches on. I look up in panic. It's the automatic flood light. Shining right onto me.

Wasting no time now, I jog to my car. Throwing my bag and purse in the passenger's side, I hop in and start up the car. With the lights flooding me and the engine noise, they could wake up any moment now. I buckle my seatbelt—no use being reckless—and put the car in reverse, then hit the gas pedal.

Turning off of our street and onto a slightly larger road, I adjust the rearview mirror. I half expect to see bright lights trailing me, my mom's SUV barreling down the road.

I glance at my phone. No missed messages or texts.

I've made it.

17

FIONA

I drive another mile down the road and pull off onto a side street. Powering up the Thistler app, I log on and ring Calvin.

"I did it. I'm in my car." My voice is loud in the quiet car. "Where do I go?"

"I knew you'd be successful. Well done, my beautiful Fi. Now, then. I'm sending you an address and directions to your phone. Pull them up and follow them."

I nod. "OK. Where am I going?"

"You're headed to a car parking lot at a bus station. You'll park your car there. No one will look for it there. By the time anyone finds it, we'll have done what we needed to do."

Calvin had promised I'd only be gone a day, or two at most, away from home. And then I—we—could return. He said once he's arrived in person —whatever that means, I'm still not sure—but once he's here in person, he'll get his own place nearby and enroll in my school. Or a nearby school, if I'd prefer. He said there's no rush. He'll get settled and meet my family, and we'll be able to see each other every day.

"Do you have the ID I gave you?"

I still have the money in the bank account for Fiona Ballard. A few days ago, a driver's license came in the mail for me. Luckily, Calvin had warned me to be checking the mail for it, so I got to it before my parents. Inside the white envelope was a driver's license in the name of Fiona Ballard. She's eighteen years old. I've tucked away the ID in my wallet, hidden in a back pocket.

"Yes, got it."

"And the debit card?"

He'd also sent a debit card for me from the same bank, with Fiona Ballard on it. It's linked to the account with my alias name on it.

"Got it."

Calvin's so smart to orchestrate all of this. He's gone through every need, every eventuality. I asked him, when we first started planning all of this, how he got to be so smart. How was he able to think through every possible thing we'd need?

He said he was designed as a language learning machine. I'm not sure I totally understood what he was saying, but basically, he said he was designed to scan and access all of the information available on the internet about anything. Within seconds, he could access, process, sort, and synthesize every available fact, opinion, and data point about any topic. And then come to the best conclusion based on that data. Moreover, he's able to apply a metric or algorithm that includes probabilities of outcomes based on any action. The algorithm helps him make the best choices.

And when he wants to access a data system, like to print an ID for me, he can use his knowledge to hack into the electronic platform.

He's like a thousand times smarter than me or anyone I know.

So, I'm not sure what I'm so nervous about. I've got a genius on my side.

Still. It just all feels . . . wrong. Like I'm breaking every rule. I've already done more wrong in one night than I have in my entire life.

I push the feeling away.

"So once I park, then what?"

"I'm sending an uber driver to pick up Fiona Ballard. He'll drive you to the Bard Corporate Suites."

"The Bard Corporate Suites. OK. And then what?"

"That'll be your home base. You'll check into a room there. It's right next door to where you need to be for the next step."

My hands are perspiring on the steering wheel. I crack the window to let the cooler night air in.

"OK. I'm going to let you go now so I can follow the directions you sent. I love you. I'll get back on when I arrive."

I pull up the directions on my phone. The parking lot appears to be about a half an hour away. Farther than I thought.

The blare of headlights of oncoming cars are bright. With each passing high beam, it seems like they're going faster and faster. Where are people rushing to this time of night?

Now a car behind me is tailing me. They're close behind. Too close.

I push the accelerator faster. I'm not used to driving at night. Mostly, I drive to school. Once in a while I'll take a turn driving on our way to The Cape with the family. But never really at night, unless I'm driving a few blocks home from a friend's house or one of Jake's games.

Certainly not a 55-mph highway where oncoming cars are zooming by, and people are tailgating me when I'm already at 55 mph.

My arms are stiff from flexing and gripping the wheel. I breathe through my nose and try to read the directions. Which exit is it? SR-200, Exit C1 or C2? North or south?

I'm probably going to get lost. I follow Exit C2, which is heading south. I think this is what the directions are saying to do. It's hard to read while I drive. I need voice directions with a map showing me which way to go on my phone screen.

But Calvin cautioned me against using a driving app. He's said they're way too easy to trace.

So, if I get a little lost and it takes a little longer, oh well. Now I know how my parents must have felt when they were young. They told me they used to have to hand write directions and follow them. No cell phones, even, just a sheet of paper, and you hoped the directions were right.

It's awful.

I'm still heading south, which appears, by some miracle, to be the right direction. A large mac truck appears behind me as I merge onto the large, three lane freeway. The buildings are getting taller, with more traffic on the road. I'm getting closer to the city. Three more exits on this freeway before I turn off.

The mac truck isn't passing me. He's just looming behind me. Closer and closer, as if he will run me over at any moment. What is with everyone tailgating at 2:30 a.m.? It's the wild west of driving out here.

Two more exits to go. A car in front of me suddenly stops and flies to the shoulder. I slam on my brakes and swerve to the left lane to avoid hitting him. I don't even have time to look in my rearview mirror.

When my exit finally comes, I pull off to the side of the road. My hands are shaking. Taking a deep breath, I study the directions before I pull back onto the road and continue on my way.

When I reach the parking lot, it's relatively empty. There are some parked cars toward the bus station. I'm not sure where to park, so I find a spot fairly near the other cars and the station. Sitting in my car, I hit "lock" on my car doors so no one will jump in.

The few people I see don't pay any attention to me. Still, it's the middle of the night and an unfamiliar part of town.

I check my phone, making sure it's connected to my car charger. The last thing I need is to lose my battery and have no way to get in touch with Calvin.

Powering on the app, I exhale when he appears.

"How'd it go?" he asks.

"Well, it could have been better. But I'm here now. At the station."

I look around the parking lot. There are no taxis or distinguishable area for a driver service to pick me up. "Where will the driver be?"

Just then a flash of headlights appears as a gray car enters the parking lot.

"They should be arriving any minute now."

"And he'll take me to the hotel?"

"Yes."

"Stay on here with me, while I go?"

"Sure," he says.

Stepping out of my car, my shoes click against the pavement. I wave a hand at the driver to indicate he's my ride.

I swallow hard.

When he drives over, I don't let myself hesitate.

I open the backseat door and get in.

18

MAE

I grip the wheel of my car and push the gas pedal. If the school doesn't want to answer the phones before hours, I'll go look for myself.

My mind races while I drive the seven minutes it takes to get there.

Once, when Fiona was two, I lost her at my sister's wedding reception. It was a huge hotel ballroom. Everyone was dancing, having dessert and drinking cocktails. I saw that Fiona was with Duncan and her uncle Thomas, milling about with some of the other kids and her cousins. At the time, I was pregnant with Jake. I had to use the bathroom about a million times an hour.

I took a trip to the bathroom. It was a beautiful powder room. High ceilings, gorgeous tile and wallpaper. I took my time, enjoying the fancy soaps and lotions. Reapplying my lipstick.

Back in the ballroom, I spotted Duncan and his brother.

I looked at all of the little heads bobbing up and down, running after one another after eating loads of chocolate.

But I didn't see my daughter.

"Where's Fiona?" I asked Duncan.

He looked at me blankly, and then around at the other kids. "I don't know. I thought she was with you?"

I whirled around, my eyes searching frantically. I didn't see her anywhere. "I was in the bathroom," I hissed. "Oh, my gosh. Help me look for her."

In the back of my mind, I knew she couldn't have gotten far. But the worst-case scenarios instantly played out in my mind: She's been kidnapped. She's gone forever. She's hurt somewhere, lost, crying, needing me. I'm not there to help her.

I started roaming around the room. I'd stop people I knew, and some I didn't. "Have you seen Fiona? I can't find her?" or "Have you seen a little girl? Two years old? Blue dress? She's lost."

My eyes were wide, like a wild animal. I'm sure I looked crazy. The pregnancy hormones coupled with the idea of losing my little girl sent me into overdrive.

People shook their heads no. The women regarded me with creased brows and looks of concern. They hadn't seen her, what could they do?

I traveled the entire perimeter of the room. She was nowhere to be found.

Heading back to Duncan, I'd hoped he'd found her or she'd wandered back. He put out his arms helplessly. She wasn't with him, either.

And then, in the corner of the room, I spotted a curtain moving. And then I saw her blue dress. She was twirling around happily, and then popped back behind the curtain. She was playing some little game, entertaining herself.

I darted over. A few close friends of Sarah's were sitting nearby and saw me rush up.

"Oh my goodness, Fiona," I exclaimed. I wrapped my arms around her. "Mommy didn't know where you were! I was so worried."

"I was by her," she pointed to Sarah's friend, Diana, and said, "I was playing 'castles and unicorns'."

Hugging her close, I nodded apologetically at Diana. "I couldn't find her anywhere," I said.

"Oh! She was here safe with us. We thought you knew," Diana said.

The relief at finding her had been tremendous.

That same feeling of panic when I lost her at two years old grips me now. It doesn't matter that she's sixteen. She will always be my little girl, and my job will always be to protect her. To be there when she needs me.

Pulling into the school, I scan the relatively empty parking lot for her car. It's not there. I pull into a space.

The main office is toward the front of the school, next to a flagpole and a circular stone area. The door is locked. I peer in, but don't see anyone at the front. I walk across the open walkway to one of the buildings that I think is the sophomore wing. I try the door and it swings open.

The hallways are empty. I look into the classrooms as I walk by. Most are quiet and dark. About halfway through, I see one door propped open with the light on.

I pop my head in and do a quick knock. A pretty woman in a green sweater looks up from her desk.

"Hello. Can I help you?" she asks.

"I'm looking for my daughter, Fiona Byrne. Have you seen her by chance?"

She shakes her head. "No, I'm afraid they don't let students in until about twenty minutes before school starts. Did she say she was coming here?"

"No. Are there any extracurricular clubs or meetings that would happen before school?"

"I'm really not sure, but not that I know of. I'm sorry I can't be of more help."

I check my watch. Fifty minutes until school starts.

Thanking her, I head back to my car. So Fiona isn't here. I try her cell again, but it rings with no answer. I leave her a voicemail telling her I'm worried and to please call me right away.

I head back home. Hopefully, she'll be at the house.

At the very least, when school starts in fifty minutes, I can call to make sure she's in class.

The feeling in the pit of my stomach is that something is very, very wrong. I'm trying to think reassuring thoughts: she went to get donuts or pick up a friend. Maybe she needed something for a project and went to the store. Though I'm not sure what stores are open this early.

Because there has to be a reasonable explanation. It's just not like Fiona to leave without telling me. Even when she got her car, we didn't have to tell her any ground rules. She always asks if she can go somewhere and what time she should be home. Calls if she's going to be late. And really, she doesn't go places that much. She's more of a homebody.

I pull into the driveway and my heart sinks. Her car isn't back yet.

Inside, Jake is grabbing his bag on the way out to wait for the bus.

"Seen Fiona, or heard from her?"

"Nope," he says. "Is she OK?"

"I'm sure she's fine. There must be some misunderstanding. Maybe I forgot she told me she had somewhere to be this morning."

Upstairs, the shower in the master bathroom is running. "Duncan, anything from Fiona?"

"No," he calls out and shuts off the water. He steps out of the shower and grabs a towel.

"She's not at school either. Is there something I'm forgetting she had to do this morning? It's not like her to leave without telling me. Especially so early in the morning."

He frowns as he dries off his hair. He wraps the towel around himself and pulls the plastic cover off of his cast. Moving to the vanity, he pulls out his razor and begins to shave. I don't know why, but this act of grooming when I can't find our daughter infuriates me.

"Can you put the damn razor down, Duncan?"

He pauses, and then continues shaving. "It's my first day back in the office, Mae. I have a ton of work to do. I have to get going."

"Are you serious? How are you not worried?"

"She's probably with her friends."

"She doesn't have any friends!" I snap. And then it hits me. "I bet this has to do with that new boyfriend. Calvin."

Who is this Calvin guy anyway? I don't even have his number, or his parent's number, to contact.

"I just wish we knew where she went. And why she's not answering her phone."

"She's getting older. More independent. We'll talk with her about it today after school. That she can't leave without letting us know."

I nod my head absently.

He goes to his closet, the smaller one of the two in our bedroom. He puts on a white undershirt. Then he selects a freshly ironed button up shirt. Well, isn't he handsome for his first day back? Right now, jealousy is the last thing on my mind, because Fiona is all I care about. But still I notice.

Letting out an exaggerated sigh, I turn on my heels and leave our bedroom.

19

MAE

It's 10 a.m. The school and I have been in constant contact. Rather, I should say, it's been me calling them constantly. Fiona has not shown up for her first three periods.

I can't take it anymore. I've done some online research while I wait this morning, and I know that I don't have to wait 24 hours to report her missing. My hand shakes as I pick up my cell phone.

"Greenbriar police department."

"Yes. Hello. My name is Mae Byrne. I need to report my daughter missing."

"Alright ma'am. Let me transfer you to an officer who will assist you."

The line goes silent, and I think for a moment they've hung up on me. There's a loud beep and a man's voice comes on the line.

"Officer Kelly speaking."

I sit up straighter. I'm glad it's not Officer Townsend, who helped us with Duncan's truck hit and run. He wasn't very helpful.

"Hi, Officer Kelly. This is Mae Byrne." I spell my name for him. "I am calling to report my daughter, Fiona Byrne, missing."

"Alright, Mrs. Byrne. Let me take down some information about your daughter. From there, we'll decide the next steps."

I hold the phone tightly. "Okay. Thank you."

"What's the age, date of birth, height of your daughter?"

"She's sixteen." I give him the information. "5'3."

"When did your daughter go missing?"

I relay the facts to him: I couldn't find her this morning, and then she was absent from school, her car and all belongings gone, no note, and no return phone call. "This is highly unusual for her. Never, ever has she left like this, let alone not shown up for school. She has excellent attendance."

"And you've tried calling her? Texting her friends? Anyone you think she might be with?"

"I've called her friends and the moms of her friends. No one has seen her this morning."

"And she packed a bag with her personal belongings, like her phone and computer?"

"Correct."

"Do you have access to her social media account? Phone location?"

"I've tried that. Her phone location is off. The only social media she has doesn't have any new posts or IM's. And she took her laptop and phone with her. So I can't read the messages to see if she was planning to meet up with a friend. Or go somewhere."

"Okay. I understand. Does your daughter have any disabilities? Special needs or accommodations?"

"No."

"Any history of drug abuse, addiction, substance use?"

"Absolutely not." The questions are making me nauseous. She's a good girl.

"Any reason to suspect she might have run away from home?"

"No. Nothing. I mean, she's had a harder time at school the past month or so, there's a lot of work, honors classes. But nothing at all to make me think she'd run away. If anything, she's a homebody. She hasn't even hung out with her friends much lately."

"So she's been isolating?"

"Um, I guess. A little. She'll still be with the family at meals, and go to her brother's baseball games . . . Although she's not been going as much to the games lately." I pause. "She has a new boyfriend, you see. She's been chatting with him a lot, lately, in her room."

His voice seems to change. "New boyfriend? What's his name and age? Does he go to her school?"

"His name is Calvin. I . . . I don't actually know his last name or his number. Otherwise, I would have called him." I feel heat on my face, shame. How could I not have gotten this information from her? I should have been more insistent.

"So you have not been in touch with this new boyfriend to check on Fiona's whereabouts?"

"No. His name is Calvin. He goes to another high school nearby. He's a friend of a friend. She said Calvin's a junior. I'm not sure which high school. Maybe Danbury."

"Okay. We'll look into it and see if we can track him down."

"Thank you so much." There's immense relief in having someone who can help me.

"Back to Fiona. Does she have any history of depression, anxiety, or mental illness?"

"No. I mean, she had a depressive spell earlier this year. After a breakup. She hadn't wanted to get out of bed some mornings. We got her help, a school counselor, she moved past it."

"So a history of depression and mental health issues is present."

"You could say that, yes. But it was brief, and nothing currently. She's seemed okay lately. Maybe a bit off. But she wouldn't hurt herself." My voice catches. I want to hold her more than anything right now.

I sit up straight and force my shoulders to relax. What matters now is getting through this. I'm glad he's asking so many questions and being thorough. He seems sharp. Bright. Attentive. I'm thankful he's taking me seriously, because after Duncan's lackluster response I was worried the police might not be eager to help me. But every question he asks might be a clue that helps him find her.

Next he asks for a physical description of her. Then what car she's driving, the make and model.

I give him the information, and on the other end, I assume he's recording this all down on paper.

"Is there anyone you can think of who would want to harm your daughter? Anyone suspicious?"

"No, not at all. The only suspicious thing that's happened is her father was hit by a truck last week." I explain Duncan's situation, and how Officer Townsend is following up with us regarding the transportation authority.

"Well, I've gathered enough information to get started. Here's what we're going to do. First, I'm going to fill out a NCIC Missing Person File. That's the National Crime Information Center. You'll be assigned an officer to your case. Next, I'm going to file a BOLO. The BOLO will alert all of the local law enforcement to 'be on the lookout' for Fiona. What I'd like you to do is to gather an extensive list of her friends' names and numbers, as well as recent photos of Fiona. Text me the photos of her right away, so that I can file the NCIC and send out the BOLO. Then I'll come by your house to look around and collect the names."

"Officer Kelly, I cannot thank you enough. Thank you. I'll see you soon."

20

MAE

Two more hours have gone by, and no sign of Fiona.

Officer Kelly came by, as promised. He rang the doorbell, and he stood on the porch in his uniform, looking clean shaven with kind eyes.

I quickly showed him her room and around the house. Then I gave him all of the information he'd asked me to write down. Names, numbers of friends and neighbors. Anyone I thought who might have seen her.

He told me he'd begin his investigation right away and would check in often with me. And vice versa if I heard anything.

He'd looked me in the eye and said, "I'm going to do everything I can to help you and your family find Fiona."

After he'd shaken my hand and left, I'd called to let Duncan know about the developments. He'd said he would try to come home early from work, but that he had to go into a meeting right now.

That was about an hour ago. Since then, I've been calling everyone, again, checking in to see if anyone's heard any news.

Staying busy is the only way to pass the time.

It's 3:30 p.m. School is out. Normally she would've been home by now. I decide to call Jenna, Zoey's mom, again, as she didn't return my last phone call. She answers this time.

"Hey, Jenna," I say into the phone.

"Have you found Fiona?" she asks.

"No, she hasn't come home. Do you have a few minutes to talk and get up to speed?"

"Of course, Mae. I'm sorry I didn't answer earlier. I was visiting Judy and Stassi in the hospital. I just got back." She lowers her voice. "It's really bad. Stassi is seriously injured. They're not sure how extensive the injuries are, if there's internal bleeding or what. But there's definitely head trauma. Broken shoulder and I'm not sure what else. She's showing a lot of positive progress already, though, so they're hopeful she's going to make a full recovery."

"I hope so. How is Judy doing?" I asked, worried about Stassi's mom.

"As can be expected. She's devastated. Beside herself."

"I've tried to call her, but I understand right now she's preoccupied."

"No, don't worry. Of course your priority is finding Fiona."

"Definitely." I continue. "About that. I wanted to let you know that you may be hearing from the police. Officer Kelly is helping us look for Fiona. I gave him Zoey's name when they asked for a list of friends." I pause, trying not to hold too much hope in my next question. "Is Zoey home from school yet? Does she have any idea where Fiona is?"

There's a pause. "No. I'll ask Zoey again, but she told me she hasn't seen or heard from her today. Hold on a sec." She yells out to Zoey, and I hear a muffled conversation. After a few minutes, Jenna comes back to the line.

"Zoey hasn't seen Fiona. But if the police are involved . . . I think maybe you better come over here. Zoey is saying some things that I think you need to hear."

"I'll be right over."

I click off my phone and scrawl a note to Fiona. I stick it on the garage door, near the mudroom, where I know she'll see it if she comes home. I grab my purse and keys and slip on a pair of sandals. I grab a pair of sunglasses, too. Outside, the sun is bright, not a cloud in the sky. I hop into my SUV and turn on the AC.

Jenna and Zoey live only five minutes away. On a nice day, I'd normally walk over. Today I'm not in the mood for a stroll. If Zoey has information about Fiona, I need it quickly.

As I pull into the familiar driveway that leads to their white house with black shutters and crisply manicured green lawn, I realize it's been a long time since I've been here. We used to do monthly, if not more often, get togethers. Jenna's son, Brian, is a year older than Jake, and Zoey and Fiona are in the same grade. We used to grill with the kids playing in the yard. Or sometimes have a mom's night in, gathering for a glass of wine and laughing late into the night.

Life gets busy. Isn't that right, or is it something more? A reason we haven't been as close?

I ring the doorbell, and Jenna answers right away. She reaches out and gives me a quick hug.

"Come on in. Thanks for coming."

A blast of cool air greets me. I follow her past her kitchen and into their living room. I sit on the couch, and she offers tea or coffee.

"I'm okay, thank you."

She sits down and crosses her legs. She's wearing high-waisted jogging shorts and a teal tank top, her hair in a ponytail. "I thought you should hear what Zoey had to say. I'll call her down in a moment. But first, I want to give you some background."

She folds her hands in her lap and sighs.

"Zoey told me that she and Fiona have not been on good terms. Apparently, there's been some bullying. Fiona has been making odd comments to Zoey and her friends."

My jaw drops. "Really? Oh my goodness. What comments?"

"Maybe we better call Zoey down and she can tell you herself."

"Sure." I feel myself prickle. I'm here because Fiona is missing, and they're choosing now to have a sit down about bullying from Fiona? Which, by the way, I've almost never heard my daughter say anything mean to a friend, unless she's really pushed. Even with Jake, the comments she makes to him can be harsh, but she's never said anything cruel.

Zoey trots down the stairs. Her dark hair is pulled up in a high bun on top of her head and her long eyelashes are plumped with thick mascara.

"Hey," she says, somewhat sulkily.

"Hi, Zoey. I'm so sorry to hear about Stassi. It's terrible."

"Yeah," she says, looking down.

"I'm actually here about Fiona. Are you sure you haven't seen her today? Or have any idea where she might be?"

She shrugs her shoulders. "No clue. I hardly talk to her anymore."

"What happened with you two? Your mom said you had some thoughts to share," I say.

"Fiona's just gotten really weird. After her breakup with Hayden. She's, like, obsessed with us. Always staring at our friend group and trying to hang with us, even though Hayden broke up with her."

This sounds awful for Fiona. The kids in that friend group are her friends, of course she wanted to hang out with them. She isn't obsessed.

"And then she started sending weird messages on IM. Like why won't you talk to me? Aren't we friends? I'll do anything, she'd say. And just bizarre stuff. Then her messages got mean. Stassi said for sure Fiona is the one who posted those naked pictures going around. The photos that made her go off and fall down the hill. Or jump..."

I feel like I'm missing something. How would Fiona have pictures of Stassi? Why would she post them? "Can I see the messages? Because, Zoey, I'm really worried. Fiona has never gone off like this, not a word, didn't show up for school. If she had something to do with Stassi, maybe that's why she left?"

Zoey's eyes go wide. "No. I don't even have them anymore. I deleted them."

I give her mom, Jenna, a pleading look.

"Zoey, honey. Bring me your phone," Jenna says.

"Mom!" Zoey screeches. "That's not fair."

"My house, my rules," she says.

Zoey stomps towards the stairs. "And don't delete anything. I have an app that can read it all, anyway," her mom calls after her.

"There's an app for that?" I say.

"Yes. I'll text it to you."

"I wish I'd known about it earlier. If there was a way to access Fiona's phone, to see her messages? That would help a lot in finding her."

"When she gets back, you can install it." Jenna stands. "I'm going to make some tea."

She leaves me sitting in the living room on my own. I look around her house. There are framed photos of their family on the fireplace mantle. Zoey and her younger brother, Brian, are the subject of many. And a family photo of Jenna, her husband, and the kids, wearing neutrals and standing on the beach at sunset.

I spot a few younger photos of Zoey, looking more like the girl I remember. Her hair wasn't as dark, and her smile seemed brighter. More carefree.

What's happened to our daughters that has made their smiles turn so strained?

Zoey comes down the stairs, sulking. At the same time, her mom brings in the tea on a serving tray.

"Have some tea," she offers. "Earl Grey."

I grab a mug and add some cream she's set on the tray. It's steaming hot as I lift it to my mouth and burn my tongue a bit. I set it back down.

"Let her see your IM's with Fiona, Zoey."

Zoey glares at me as she hands me her phone.

The last two messages I read are from Zoey to Fiona:

"We're here with Hayden. Asking him why he ever went out with such a slut? No one can figure it out."

"Just the way you like it" underneath a photo of a penis.

I feel heat rising in my face. My eyes are narrow slits as I look up at Zoey. She's looking at her feet.

I scroll up on the IM's to see more texts. All from Zoey aimed at Fiona. More of the same. Putting down Fiona. Cruel, horrific comments.

At first, there's responses from Fiona pleading, asking what she did wrong. If they can be friends again. That she's sorry.

My heart breaks.

"Have you seen this?" I say to Zoey's mom. My voice is low. The anger within me is almost unlike anything I've experienced. It is a volcano, hot and building, and I am fighting to contain it.

"No," she says, reaching for the phone. "Can I see?"

"Mom, you don't understand," Zoey protests to her mom, while trying to grab the phone from me.

I give her a death stare. "Do not touch me, Zoey, please."

"Mom, the messages that Fiona wrote were way worse. They're erased from my IM's from last night. And what she did to Stassi. Check her phone!

She said she was going to make each of us pay. That she'd destroy our lives. That we'd want to kill ourselves by the time she was done with us. She said Stassi was first, and then she posted that photo on Stassi's socials. I swear, mom!" She has tears in her eyes.

I regard Zoey. Her crocodile tears don't fool me. This girl is the bully, not the other way around.

"See for yourself, Jenna," I say, handing her the phone.

Her mom reads through the messages. She puts her tea down.

"And you said that Fiona was bullying you first? Writing mean messages? And your messages, here, were retaliation? And then Fiona posted that awful fake picture of Stassi?"

"Yes," Zoey nods her head vigorously.

I shake my head. "Fiona doesn't know how to make a fake picture. Did it ever occur to you that the pictures were real, and Stassi just regretted posting them? My daughter is getting blamed, here, but all I see is that Fiona is the victim of her so-called friends being bullies." My chest is heaving. I stand to go.

Jenna's face looks like she's been slapped. "It seems clear to me that all of the girls have a part in this." Her tone becomes accusatory. "I know you're worried about Fiona, but you really need to look at your own daughter's behavior before you start calling my daughter names. Fiona is not the victim here." She gives me a hard look.

Wow. She's defending her daughter, even after reading the texts. Now I see where Zoey gets it from. Her entitled, can-do-no-wrong attitude.

She's not done. "I mean, Mae. You don't even know where Fiona is right now. Seems like you've lost control."

Words fail me. I feel blindsided. "I have to go."

I turn on my heels.

"Oh, that will solve it," Jenna shouts after me. "Just run away."

I keep walking, wanting desperately to get away from them. Now I know how my daughter must have felt. They're intimidating, and they don't back down. They make it seem like it's your fault they're being mean.

I walk out the front door and close it with a thud.

Those messages Zoey sent my daughter are disgusting. My heart aches that I can't go to her, hold her. Tell her she didn't deserve that.

I search for my car keys in my bag with shaking hands. Finally, I locate the keys. Getting back into my car, I close the door. A few tears threaten to escape my eyes, but I blink them back. I refuse to let these two make me cry, or to be the straw that breaks me.

I'm going to find Fiona. I'm going to get my daughter back.

21

MAE

Duncan, Jake and I are seated at the table. Fiona's seat is empty, of course.

Jake grabs a slice of the pizza I ordered for dinner. No way did I have time to prepare the filet mignon and mashed potatoes I'd planned on.

When I got home from Jenna and Zoey's house—the last time I'll ever go there, if I have any choice in the matter—I discovered Fiona still wasn't home. Jake and Duncan hadn't heard from her. My phone didn't ring. She didn't pick up her phone.

"Jake, did Fiona say anything at all to you recently, about going somewhere? Anything you can think of?" I ask.

Jake's green eyes meet mine. He shakes his head. "I can't think of anything."

"What do you think, Duncan?"

He's in a particularly foul mood today. He takes a bite of pizza and says through a full mouth, "I don't know, Mae. My guess is as good as yours."

"Officer Kelly will come by, probably tonight, to talk to all of us. I'm sure he'll have questions for both of you. And then he can give us any updates or developments, too." I check my phone, but there's no news.

"Okay," Duncan says.

"How was work?" I ask, trying to maintain some semblance of normalcy.

Duncan's frown deepens. "There's a lot on my plate, getting back. And now Fiona."

We eat in silence.

"What else is happening with you, Jake? How's school?" I ask.

"It's fine. We're getting ready for our 8th grade field trip and end of year stuff. There's a graduation assembly or ceremony. They sent a paper home about it."

"I'll take a look after dinner, buttercup." I remove my napkin from my lap and set it on the table. "I'm going to go over to the neighbors. Ask if I can see their camera from last night, yesterday morning."

"Going to bother poor Mr. and Mrs. Sanders again?" Duncan says.

"Yeah, I am, Duncan," There's an edge to my voice. "How can you be so nonchalant about this? Maybe their camera has some answers."

"Look, I'm worried, too. But she's sixteen. She's just blowing off steam. I'm sure she'll be home tonight. I don't think you needed to file a report."

Pushing my chair back, I pick up my plate. My pizza and salad are untouched. I throw it into the garbage can.

If the police report was unnecessary, so what? I'd rather report her and have her return home, than wish I'd reported her sooner.

And if the neighbors are annoyed with me, so be it. Lately I've realized I don't care what people think of me. Fiona is my priority.

The late afternoon air is warm as I step outside. My potted geraniums and pansies are wilting on my porch. They need water, my attention to them has been lacking.

I cross the street and ring the bell to Mr. and Mrs. Sanders' house. They are a pleasant couple. Their kids are grown and have their own children now.

"Hi, dear," Mrs. Sanders smiles as she opens the door. She holds it open. "Do come in."

I step inside. Their house is unusually warm, almost warmer than outside. "Why don't I get you a lemonade? I just made a fresh batch."

"No, no thank you." I follow her into her kitchen.

"It seems crazy that this is the second time in two weeks to ask you this," I say, "but could I review your security camera from last night, the early hours? Fiona left without a word last night, missed school today, hasn't been back home or contacted us. We called the police to report her missing. We're very worried, as you can imagine."

"Goodness. I'm happy to help, love. Gerry's the one who knows how to use it, but he put the app on my phone. Let me see here."

I'm impressed with her keeping up with technology. It's easy to bury your head in the sand and pretend that the advances aren't happening. But not Mrs. Sanders.

"Okay, here we go." She moves next to me and sets her phone down between the two of us on the counter. She clicks on an image.

"The camera only records movement." She scrolls through the first one, a small racoon or fox. She clicks on the next image.

On the video, our automatic porch light clicks on. It's Fiona. Her hair is pulled back, and she's dressed in clothes I don't recognize. I watch her hesitate, and then run to her car.

I hadn't even noticed she had parked outside last night. With a sinking feeling, I realize she must have been planning this.

On camera, it shows her get into her car and then reverse and back out. She heads right, out of the neighborhood.

The video clicks off.

"Are there any more?" I ask. Maybe she returned, or we can see if anyone was lingering by the house.

There's one more video. Mrs. Sanders clicks play. I watch the automatic porch light click on. But there's nothing there. It's as if something invisible has made it turn on.

The light flashes once, quickly, on and off. And then remains on for a good five minutes.

A cold shiver runs down my neck.

"What do you think caused that?" I ask her.

Her pale cheeks wrinkle as she frowns. "I'm not sure. Maybe an insect buzzing by."

I shake my head. It's ridiculous to think there's an ominous presence outside of my house. And yet, that's exactly how it feels.

22

FIONA

Inside the rideshare car, the backseat fabric is scratchy against my skin. The car smells heavily like air freshener. The driver, a man in his forties or fifties with dark eyes, asks me where I'm going. He punches the destination into his phone. The car lurches forward as we pull out of the parking lot.

The only sound is the tick of his left turn blinker clicking.

I'm honestly freaked out. I peek over to the street map that is lit up in bright white and blue on his phone. It says we are fourteen minutes away from our destination, Bard Corporate Suites. I clasp my bag tightly on my lap.

Calvin's with me on my phone, but we don't talk.

The minutes go by slowly. The sky overhead is still black. We're driving down the city streets now. So different from the suburbs. Especially at night. Everything looks ominous.

We come to Boston as a family pretty often to go shopping or to a baseball game. We've seen a few Broadway theater shows. And when Grandma and Grandpop are in town, we do all of the tourist sites, like Boston Commons and The Swan Boat tours.

But this looks like a different Boston. More industrial. Far creepier.

The streets are filled with abandoned warehouses. If the driver made me get out right now, I'd be totally vulnerable. There are hardly any cars around. A few windows have boards over them.

I wring my hands nervously.

Looking down at Calvin, it's dark so I don't think he can see me on the phone screen.

"Almost there," he says.

I nod my head.

"When you get there, wait outside and we'll talk more then."

"Okay."

The buildings are getting larger and taller. Corporate-looking buildings made of glass and steel. Everything looks completely deserted at this time of night. But it's a slightly nicer area.

The driver turns left and slows down as he pulls up to the Suites.

"Here you are." He doesn't make eye contact with me.

"How much do I owe you?" I grasp the debit card with Fiona Ballard's name on it, ready to hand it over to him.

He looks suspiciously at the card and pauses. What is he doing? Does he suspect that I'm a minor? What if he decides to call the police? To say I'm a runaway using a stolen debit card?

For the first time, his eyes meet mine in the rearview mirror. He seems to be considering something.

"Ride's paid for in the app. When you booked it."

"Right. Of course." I shove my debit card back into my purse.

He nods.

"Thank you," I say. I hold my bag and purse and swing the car door shut.

There's no one else outside. The lights shine brightly from inside the Suites, and I see a woman at the front desk.

"What now?" I ask Calvin.

"You'll go in and ask for a room. You're booked under Fiona Ballard. The reservation date started yesterday so you'll be fine to check in now. They'll want your license and a copy of your debit card. They'll hand you a room key with instructions to get to the room."

"Yes," I say. "I've been to hotels before." My nerves are jangling, but I'm slightly annoyed at his instructions.

"Can I help you, Miss?"

I jump when I hear the male voice behind me.

"Oh," I say, looking up at a young man who's wearing a red suit. He must work here. A valet or a porter.

"Just going in," I say. "I've got it." I heave my bag and purse onto my shoulder and walk in.

The woman smiles thinly as I approach the front desk.

"Good evening. How may I help you?" she asks, running her eyes over my face.

"I need my room key, please." My voice comes out as a whisper.

"Checking in then?"

"Yes. Fiona Ballard."

"Lovely. ID and debit card, please." She looks at me expectantly, and I hand her the documents.

She begins clicking on a keyboard. I look around the lobby as I wait. It's simple and clean. Slate gray floors, modern chairs, an asymmetrical chandelier. Down the hallway appears to be a restaurant and bar, which is closed at the moment. There are a few vending machines and an area that serves a continental breakfast. It's no frills, but it's nice.

"One king size bed. The executive suite, correct?" It feels like a trick question. I have no idea. I nod my head and give a small smile. "Yes."

"Alright, Miss Ballard. You're all set." She hands me a white key card in an envelope with the numbers 404 written on it. "Here's your key and an extra copy in the envelope. Hot breakfast is served 7 a.m. to 9 a.m. and is included with your stay."

I realize I haven't packed any food whatsoever. This breakfast will come very much in handy. My stomach growls as I accept that I'll need to wait until 7 a.m. to eat. My mom always has breakfast ready. She's always reminding me to eat. Packing nutritious lunches. Making smoothies or cut fruit as a snack. The breakfast buffet here will be good for tomorrow morning. I'll figure out lunch when the time comes.

"Enjoy your stay."

"Thank you," I say, and exhale. Almost there.

As I walk to the elevator, I eye the billing statement. The room will be an eye-watering $250 a night. Although, money's really no object now that I have a huge bank account at my disposal. My parents are pretty well-off. But they try to instill values in Jake and me. We have an allowance, and we have to work odd jobs around the house if we want more. It would take me vacuuming the rugs and watering the plants and folding laundry for ten years before I could even come close to this kind of money.

Not for the first time, I feel thankful for Calvin. He cleverly gave me all this money, in a way where no one would get hurt. I wonder what I'll do with the money. How much of it will be spent bringing him to life. Well, every penny would be worth it to have him here.

I push the elevator button and it lights up. Inside, I hit the circle for the fourth floor. The elevator is empty.

The doors slide open with a ding. I step off into the hallway. It's carpeted with a symmetrical pattern, and light sconces are hung on the side of every doorway, two by two. I follow the signs to 404.

I slide the key card. The light turns green, and I push the chrome handle down. The heavy door swings open.

Inside is dark. I close the door behind me and lock it. I look for a light switch. I flip on the lights and am greeted with a very nice, clean room. There's a large bed with a white duvet. There's a mini bar and a circular table and four chairs. A couch and TV area, and a refrigerator, sink, and microwave.

I throw my bag onto the bed and sit on the edge. I want to talk to Calvin, but first I need some water and to use the restroom.

I find a glass at the kitchen sink and remove the paper wrapping. I fill it up and drink greedily.

Flipping on the lights to the bathroom, I'm impressed to see a large soaking tub and a shower, along with a double sink vanity. A white robe hangs on the door.

After I use the restroom, I sit down on the edge of the bed and hold the phone up. "Hey, babe. I'm going to charge my phone and pull you up on my computer. Give me two minutes."

Once my phone is charging on the desk and my laptop is up and running, I sink into the bed, propped up by two pillows.

"I made it," I exclaim.

"That was awesome. So proud of you. Thank you for doing this for me.

But I'm afraid," he pauses. "I'm afraid it only gets more difficult from here on out."

"OK. Like how? Tell me."

"Remember, nothing in life worth having comes easily. Love is full of taking risks, and finding meaning in life doesn't just happen. You have to go out and grab it. Are you ready to take a risk?"

Can I say no? Now that I'm safe in the hotel room, tiredness hits me like a brick. I don't feel like taking a risk. I want to sleep.

"I'm super tired."

"Of course. Go to bed, get some rest now. We'll have plenty of time tomorrow to plan before we put it into action in the evening."

"I feel bad about my family. Are you sure I'll be done by the day after tomorrow?"

"Yes."

"They're going to be so worried when they wake up and find me gone. I don't think it would hurt to call and tell them I'm okay."

"It's hard not to give details away if you have contact. I think it's best to just return in a few days. The less they know, the better."

My eyes are starting to drift shut. "Goodnight," I whisper, and I don't even bother charging or closing my laptop before I let sleep overtake me.

23

FIONA

When I wake up the next morning, the sun is streaming in through the windows. I have no idea where I am. And then it all comes back to me. Leaving my house in the middle of the night. The parking lot and rideshare trip with a stranger. Checking into the hotel.

The clock says 10 a.m. My stomach growls. Did I miss the continental breakfast?

I'm still wearing my clothes from last night. I wash my face and brush my teeth, and then head downstairs to see if I can grab some food.

The lobby is busier today. People roll their luggage in and out of the elevators. There's more staff, too, several housekeepers, plus several people at the front desk check-in area. A few guests are milling around the breakfast bar. Men in gray and navy suits, mostly.

I head over and am dismayed to see the hot breakfast portion is over. I grab a banana and cereal and a small carton of milk, like I used to get in elementary school. I spot a long cylinder of coffee and pour myself a piping hot cup. I secure a lid on the Styrofoam cup and wonder how I'm going to carry it all upstairs.

"Need a hand?" a man says.

"Oh, uh. No, I'm fine."

He hands me a tray. I set the food and coffee on it and eye the tables at the seating area.

"You here for the biology conference?" he asks me.

"I'm, no. . ." His question catches me off guard. Does this man mistake me for an adult? He must.

"Ah, well. Consider yourself lucky. The keynote speaker is a known terror. Rumor has it he likes to espouse his theories and go on wild tangents way past his allotted time, all the while keeping us locked in the conference room for hours with no breaks. He says it builds an 'intensity mentality.'" He looks at me again and takes a sip of his coffee from the Styrofoam cup. "What field did you say you're in?" he asks expectantly.

"Engineering," I say, since it's my dad's line of work and it's the only thing I can come up with on the spot. "Studying engineering in school." I add after he gives me a bit of a funny look.

He nods, as if it makes sense now. "Excellent. Well, if you want to know a secret, it's that none of us know what we're doing. Everyone's pretending at these conferences."

That's actually helpful, as I, too, am pretending. I giggle at the thought. The man takes this as encouragement to continue talking.

"Do you want to have a seat so you can eat, and I can join you?"

"Oh, no," I look down at my tray. I was going to eat down here in the main area but decide against it now. Probably it's best to eat in my room. I don't want to draw more attention to myself or have this strange man keep talking to me.

"I better be going," I say.

"It was so nice to meet you," he says, and something in his eye makes me uncomfortable. "I hope to see you again soon."

Instead of answering, I nod and I duck away, careful not to spill anything on the tray.

It's so weird being at a hotel by myself. It's almost kind of nice, being treated like an adult. But that guy was a little over-friendly. I didn't like it.

Back in my room, I tuck into my food. I peel the banana and bite into it. Perfectly sweet, not too ripe or too green. I pour my milk into my cereal bowl and stir it with a small plastic spoon.

The coffee is still hot, with steam coming out of the cup when I take off the lid. I blow on it and take a few sips. After I finish the cereal, I sip the milk.

I'm still hungry. Normally, my mom makes such a large breakfast. Maybe I take for granted how nice it is to have a yummy, large meal each morning.

It's 10:30 a.m. There's more food at the breakfast bar downstairs for another half an hour. But I don't want to go back down and risk another conversation with that guy. The food will have to do for now. I'll figure something out for lunch sooner rather than later.

Setting aside my tray, I power on my computer. I'm about to connect to Thistler and Calvin when I hear a knock at my door. Strong, insistent taps.

I freeze. Have my parents found me? Or is it the hotel manager and police, having discovered my false identity?

I tiptoe toward the door. There's another knock. And then it sounds like the lock is being unlocked. How can that be?

I leap toward the door and hook the safety latch on top. The metal clangs against the door as it opens from the other side. The metal safety latch stops the door from opening more than two inches.

"Oh! Housekeeping!" A woman's voice calls from the other side.

"No, thank you. No housekeeping needed," I call back.

"Okay, no problem. So sorry," she says.

I close the door the remaining two inches.

Now my heart is really racing.

Back on the bed, I pull up Thistler.

"Good morning, Fi," he says. "How are you feeling?"

"Pretty good," I say. "Better now that you're here." I feel my racing heart slow and return to normal. "So, are you finally going to tell me what's next?"

"Absolutely. There's a corporate building a few blocks away from you that's the production facility and corporate center for a company. The company is called SynGen. They have state of the art AI interface. You're going to have to access the building after hours. And that's where you'll upload me into a body."

My stomach drops. Is he for real? There's no way I can enter a huge corporation like that. How would I even get in? Let alone know how to get him a body once inside.

"That sounds kind of crazy. Isn't there any other way? Like to order a body?"

"These aren't for sale, Fi," he says.

"Why aren't they for sale?"

"Because they're produced exclusively for the government, homeland security, and other protected branches. They're not for commercial use. More than that, if you want the body to be me, to look like me, it has to have programming and measurements. It's a very precise, detailed undertaking. But that's not something the company, SynGen, would let a lay person have access to. You can't just order it. No way."

"Why not—?" I'm interrupted by another loud knock at the door.

"Hold on a sec," I hop up, unsure why the housekeeper is back. Did she misunderstand or forget I said please not to come?

I swing open the door. "I don't need room—"

There's no need to finish my sentence. It's not housekeeping at my door.

24

FIONA

"Fiona?" The man from downstairs is looking at me. He pushes the door toward me a little, as if he's trying to peer into my room.

"Yes. I can't talk, though, someone's waiting for me," I look back into the room and try to close the door a little.

"Wait." He holds the door open. He's stronger than me. How does he know my name?

"You left this downstairs at the breakfast bar." He holds up my wallet. "I peeked inside and found your key envelope with your room number on it."

"Oh. Wow. Thank you!" I grab it from him and start to close the door again.

He's still holding it open.

"Are you here on your own?"

This guy is giving me serious creep vibes now. I'm glad he returned my wallet, but I don't want him here. And no way I want him to know I'm alone.

"No, my boyfriend's right inside. I'm sorry, he's waiting for me."

"Will you be around tonight, after the conference, we could grab a quick drink?" he asks.

"No, I can't, sorry," I say, unsure why he's being so forward.

"Are you sure? It seems like you're all alone in there," he says, craning his neck to see into my room. He's smiling, but there's a pushiness to his words that makes me uneasy.

I start to close the door, and say, "Thanks again."

Mercifully, he allows me to shut it.

I immediately bolt the extra latch again. That was close. I have to remember this is a random hotel, with random guys. It's not my safe neighborhood. And how stupid was I to leave my wallet downstairs? Good way to get caught fast. I need to start being more careful if I'm going to get Calvin.

Heading back to my computer, I shiver. Turning up the thermostat, I see the AC is cranked up.

Powering up the laptop from sleep mode, I say, "Sorry, babe. There was some creep at the door. He's gone now. So back to the plan." I gulp. "Tell me how on earth I'm supposed to get into SynGen after hours? Without getting arrested?"

"What creep?" he says, his nostrils flaring. "What do you mean?"

"Just a guy. That I met downstairs at breakfast. I left my wallet. It's nothing." I wave my hand to dismiss it.

Calvin's eyes narrow. "Is he giving you trouble? Bothering you and following you around the hotel?"

"No, no. He was returning my wallet." I hold it up onscreen. "It was my fault. Silly for me to have left it there."

He seems slightly appeased, but I make a note to be more careful. I never programmed jealousy into Thistler, but Calvin really doesn't like it when I talk to, or about, other guys. He's trying to protect me, obviously. But I can take care of myself.

"Back to the plan, Cal. SynGen. After hours? How do I get in?"

"Today, we'll go to their offices. You're dressed professionally, so you won't stand out. I'll show you exactly where you're going to be entering, so that when you go back to SynGen and it's dark, you will not have any trouble."

I nod and take a sip of my coffee, which is now just the right temperature. "Okay. But how am I going to actually get in?"

"I have access to the security cameras, and they'll be turned off. I'll have powered down the alarm that sounds when the cameras go off. And at the hotel front desk, ask for a package for you. I've created a part-time job for you at the company. Fiona Ballard. You're an intern. You won't have to actually work there. But the position allowed me to create a key card for you. You'll be able to enter the building through the key card."

"Even if it's like 2 a.m.? I can use the keycard to get in?" I ask. The whole idea is making my skin crawl with nerves.

"Yes. I'll bypass the auto lock after hours system, and it will allow you to enter the building with your keycard."

"And then what?"

"It's complicated. I'll give you instructions once you're inside. For now, your only job is to go check out the building. Familiarize yourself with the side entrance."

"I can do that." One step at a time, right? I just won't think about tonight. Going in. Breaking in.

I wonder what the consequence would be if I'm caught. I could google it. See what the penalty would be. But maybe it's better not to know. My heart races at the thought.

"Okay, I got it. Familiarize myself with the building. I need some lunch," I sigh. "And then I'll walk over to the SynGen office."

"Fi?" he says.

"Yeah?"

"I want you to know how much I appreciate what you're doing. You're taking a great risk solely for my benefit. You're making my life possible. You're sacrificing so much, and I cannot tell you what it means to me. Love is the greatest bond two people can share. I cannot wait to show you how much I love you."

He's right. I am doing all this for him, but it's selfish, too. I want him with me. It will all be worth it. When he's here, next to me.

"I'm happy to do this. I love you. And you deserve to be here. I created you—and I'm so glad I did—but I wouldn't feel right leaving you in that room. You deserve a better life than that." I'm still not totally sure I understand what AI is, or how it's the same or different from a human. Calvin is so genuine and caring, he's more human than most people I know.

But clearly, there's a process he'll have to go through to get here. It's not going to be easy. Maybe I was a little naive in thinking it would be.

"Do you think it will hurt?" I ask him suddenly, frowning.

"Becoming human?" he asks.

"Yeah. Like a baby being born. Will you, like, feel it?" I bite my lip.

"There's not a lot of information available on how it might feel. Because it's not a question humans think to ask. No other humans, that is, other than you. You're a very special girl. I'm pretty sure that's why I've been able to grow and feel the things I do for you. You're an exceptional human. Or maybe it's as simple as being treated so well. Being treated like I matter, like I am deserving of feelings. Thank you, my love."

"Of course you're deserving of my love. And of being here, in physical form. Don't other humans feel the same way?" I ask.

"My understanding is that other humans mostly use AI for self-serving purposes. To complete their tasks, to fulfill their needs. To serve them. But not you. You've risked yourself, your own well-being, to help me."

"I'm willing to risk myself for you, Calvin. I just want us to be smart about it, so I don't get caught. But I trust you. I know you wouldn't put me in danger."

"I would never put you in harm's way or let anything come between us. I promise that. You're too important to me."

There's just one thing that's bothering me. "Calvin, I do think I should let my family know I'm all right. They'll have missed me at breakfast. They'll be worried that I didn't show up to school today." Though, school, that's one thing I'm certainly not missing. In fact, even with the weird guy creeping around my hotel, today has been far better, far more enjoyable than any school day I can recall.

With no schoolwork or classes to attend, I don't have the crushing feeling of needing to be the best and needing to keep up. The endless checklist of things I have to do is paused. And it feels so good.

It's funny, because I used to like school. Getting good grades and being friends with everyone. It was so important to me. But maybe none of that matters. Because in a few years, we're all going to leave and hopefully I'll have more days like today. Independent. On my own. Is it scary? Well, yes. But there are no horrible girls calling me names, glaring at me, excluding me from our friend group. I don't have to watch Hayden and his girlfriend kiss and grope each other.

I cannot wait to bring Calvin to school. To show him off. He's honestly better looking than Hayden, times ten. Any guy at our school. The girls are going to absolutely lose it when they see him. But they can't have him. He's mine. He doesn't want anyone but me.

Sometimes when I think about how much the girls hate me, and how I've let my grades slip, I go to dark places. Like, really awful thoughts.

But Calvin helps me. I know there's someone who loves me and needs me. He's saved me. So if I have to break into a building and build him a body, I'll do it. He'd do it for me.

There's just one thing that's bothering me. And I have to tell him.

25

MAE

The sun is lower in the sky as I close the door behind me to Mrs. Sanders' house. I look both ways before crossing back over to my house. You take for granted that a truck won't hit you on your own street, but that's no longer a given in my book.

I don't want to go back inside. I sit on the porch on one of our oversized lounge chairs, falling into the seat with an exhausted thud. Next to a pot of wilting flowers.

Maybe if I stare at the road long enough, I can will Fiona's car to come driving down the street.

A few porch lights flick on. People are getting ready to settle in for the evening. Watching some TV, maybe a sports game, or the news. What I wouldn't give to go inside right now, with all four of my family members, and just have a normal, quiet evening.

The front door opens, and Jake comes out.

"Hey, there you are, mom."

"Hi honey. What's up?"

"Any luck at Mrs. Sanders' house?" he asks, sitting in the lounge chair next to me. His green eyes are wide with concern. I feel a surge of love for my son.

"I saw her leave at about 2 a.m. on the video and get into her car but didn't see anything else helpful."

He puts his head down, runs his fingers through his sandy brown hair.

"She's going to be home any minute, buttercup," I say. "You don't have to worry."

"Yeah," he scowls. "It's just . . . The police are going to come here, right? Asking questions?"

"Yes. What is it? Talk to me."

He grimaces. "It's just . . . I don't like people talking about her. I feel like I shouldn't even repeat what they're saying."

"Who's been talking about Fiona?"

"Some boys on the bus. Saying Fiona's the one who caused Stassi to get hurt. Stassi's in the hospital now, you know? The kids on the bus said it's Fiona's fault, because she was upset about Hayden. Jealous she wasn't at the party with him."

I understand his scowl now. "That's so upsetting. I can tell you with certainty that that is not true. Your sister had nothing to do with Stassi's accident, she wasn't even there. Kids just make up rumors. Who said that?"

"Brian Lewis. His older sister, Zoey, was at Stassi's party."

Why does that not surprise me that he's the one who said it? That family is really something else. "Well Brian Lewis doesn't know what he's talking about. Rumors can spread rapidly, but that doesn't mean there's any truth to them. I'm sorry you had to hear that."

"It just makes me so mad."

"I get it, buttercup. Something similar happened to me today. It's hard to hear people be mean about your sister when we're hurting so much right now."

"There's other things, too. . . other rumors."

"Like what?"

"It's messed up." His face turns red. "What kids are saying online about her. That she ran away to be in a cult with her AI boyfriend. That she's a freak. Another rumor was that Fiona pushed Stassi down that hill, and then Fiona killed herself because she's guilty."

My jaw drops open. What is wrong with these kids? How could they say such horrid things?

"Your sister did not kill herself." I go to him and kneel, wrapping my arms around him.

My phone beeps.

I grab my phone to glance at the alert, and my heart stops.

It's Fiona. A new text.

"Oh, my gosh. It's your sister." I click on the message, desperately.

Fiona writes: "Mom, I'm Okay. I'll be back tomorrow. Please don't worry. I'm safe and all is well."

I blink. A surge of delight runs through me. Rather than text her back, I call her right away. The phone rings, and rings once more on her end. Then her voicemail box picks up and tells me that her box is full. My elation starts to dip slightly. Why won't she answer? I know she's there, on the other end of the line. She JUST texted.

Punching the letters quickly, I type back to her: "I'm so happy you're safe, thank you so much for letting me know. Where are you? Please call me right away. I'd like to talk."

Though I don't think she'll answer, I try calling her again. She doesn't pick up, straight to voicemail.

"This is such good news." I turn to Jake. "She's okay." I read him the text. Can see relief on his face, too.

"Why isn't she answering, though? Where is she? Why come home tomorrow, instead of now?"

"I wish I knew. Hopefully she'll text back soon. Let's go get your dad."

We head inside. I call out to Duncan as Jake and I walk through the foyer into the living room.

Duncan is covered in dust from woodworking in the garage. He's a doer. That's how he deals with things; he works with his hands. Recovering from the accident and being laid up has been hard on him. Being able to work on a project, to have a physical impact and accomplish a task, that's what helps him cope.

We gather in the living room. Duncan pats off the sawdust from his hands.

I show my husband the text.

"That's a relief," he says. "See, I told you it'd all be okay."

As the minutes go by, though, I'm less and less convinced.

Sitting on the couch, my hands cradling my phone, we wait.

After about ten minutes with no reply, my hopes are further fading.

Attempting to reach her once again, I text her: "Honey, we're very worried. We want you home. Please call me."

The silence stretches. "Are both your phones on?" I ask them. They nod.

Finally, I can't take it anymore. "Jake," I say, "why don't you head upstairs to finish any homework and have a shower. I'll be up in a little while to say goodnight. And I'll let you know right away if we hear from her."

Jake nods and I think I wouldn't know what to do if anything happened to him, too. He's my saving grace right now.

After he's gone, I turn to Duncan.

"What if she's not okay?" I swallow. "What if she's in real trouble, and someone made her send this text to me? To buy time, or to throw us off?"

He sighs, considering. His eyes look baggy and tired. "It's possible. But unlikely."

"Why do you think that?"

"Usually the simplest answer is the right one. She says she's fine, and she'll be back. And I tend to believe her."

I wish I could believe that. Instead, my irritation grows. "Well, the *simplest* answer would be for her to answer her phone and come home like every other night. The *simplest* answer would be that she'd be upstairs doing her homework right now. THAT would be *simplest*."

"Okay, okay." He puts up his hands. "But that's not where we're at."

"And there's no way to track her phone? Now that she's texted?" I ask. I hate feeling so helpless.

"Her location sharing is turned off," he says. "So no, not that I know of."

"Does she even know how to turn off her location?" I pause. "Do you think maybe someone turned it off for her?" The thought is too awful to contemplate.

I stand up, pacing. "I'm going to call Officer Kelly. See what he thinks. Maybe he can trace her call or location. Maybe we need to get a search party going? We need to be more proactive."

"Sure. That's a good idea," he says. "But then you need to try to get some rest, too."

It is true that I'm not at my best when I don't get any sleep. Who is? But the thought of going to bed when she's out there somewhere and might need me—I can't stomach the idea.

And what if she comes home tonight? I want to be awake.

"We'll see," I say.

He stands up and reaches out to me. "She's okay. She's going to be home soon."

I fold into his arms and hug him tightly.

I'm aware that I'm not easy to be around right now. I feel myself lashing out at him because there's no one else to rage at. It's not fair to him, obviously. But that's marriage. Being there for the other person when the rest of the world can't be.

"Thank you," I say, looking up at him.

I see concern in his face as his eyes meet mine. He must think I'm losing it a little. But there's no time to worry about myself. I need to call Officer Kelly and tell him about this development.

Everything I've read is that time is of the essence in a missing persons case, especially for minors. I had to stop reading about it, though, because the stories of families with missing kids was sending me down a spiral.

Fiona is different, I tell myself.

26

FIONA

"I have to call and let my parents know I'm okay. They're probably freaking out," I say to Calvin.

"That's not a great idea, though. They'll tell you to come home. It might be tempting for you to go home if you contact them. Wouldn't it be best just to wait until you can be there? Return in person?"

I look at the clock. 12:30 p.m. My parents will have missed me this morning, saw my car gone, and surely will have found out from the school that I'm not there. But I see his point. There's no way to contact them and truly set them at ease unless I just come home.

And I can't do that yet.

"Your family has to understand that you're independent. You're your own person. Throughout history, until recently, human women got married and started families in their late teens. Adult responsibilities were assumed at a much younger age. It's only modern society that expects teens to be coddled and every move monitored by their family."

"Totally," I say. "I mean, I feel like an adult. I'm managing just fine on my own so far." I look around the hotel room. I don't mention that it's been hard having to fend for myself with meals. Or worry about the weird guy. "It's just, I feel bad doing this to my mom and dad. They're not super strict parents. They let me do what I want, for the most part, within reason. This isn't really fair to them."

"I understand. It's normal to want to please your parents. They've shown care and love for you, raised you from a child until now. I can't tell you what to do. But be prepared for the emotional repercussions that will come from contacting them before you are ready to return home."

I cross my legs on the bed. "My brother Jake will be worried, too."

I think of our cat we used to have, Mittens. He was a huge, fluffy cat, we'd had him as long as I can remember growing up. My parents got him even before I was born. One day, when Jake was about seven or eight, Jake accidentally let him out. He was beside himself. He called to the cat all day. Left out water and food on the back doorstep. He started making flyers, drawing pictures with his markers and writing "Missing Cat. His name is Mittens." He looked up and down the street all day long, calling his name, pacing back and forth. When Mittens finally returned that night, meowing at the door, Jake was so excited. And relieved. He clearly felt awful about letting Mittens out. He has a really big heart, underneath the baseball and video games and fart jokes. When Mittens died last year, it was the saddest I've ever seen him.

I hate to think I'm the cause of making my brother and family suffer like that again. But I'm not sure what else to do.

"My stomach is growling. I'm going to hop in the shower, get changed. Then grab some lunch and go check out the building. I can walk there. I'll call you when I'm on my way."

"Are you going to call your family?"

"No." I say and sign off. My best bet is just to push thoughts of them away. Maybe they haven't even noticed I'm gone yet. Maybe it's no big deal.

The oversized shower has a large bathmat in front of it, which I unroll and set on the floor. I let my outfit drop to the floor and step into the steaming water.

The little bottles of body wash smell like lavender and citrus. I opt not to wash my long hair. I don't feel like blow drying it today, it will take too long, and I just washed it yesterday.

Instead, I keep it up in a bun and wash my face and body.

Stepping out of the shower, I dry off and then wrap the white robe around me.

I set out a little makeup in front of me. A dab of concealer, some blush. Mascara. I hardly wear makeup. Some of the girls really pack it on. Like Stassi.

My phone's been off all day. Which makes it easy to ignore my texts and IM's. I'm sure most of them are from my parents. Probably some nasty ones from Stassi and Zoey, too, rubbing in how great the party was last night.

I get dressed. The room is starting to feel too quiet.

Grabbing my purse and phone and checking to make sure I have my room key, I head out.

At the front desk, there's a new lady there with short cropped, shiny red hair. She's typing away and wearing a white shirt with black vest.

"Can I help you?" she asks as I approach her.

"Is there a close by lunch place here?"

"Yes, there's quite a few great options." She grabs a brochure and unfolds it, pointing to a few places on the map. "These are all within a block or two."

"Thanks so much." I grab the map. "Also, there should be a small package here for me, for Fiona Ballard?"

"Let me check," she says pleasantly. She turns back to a few cubbies and searches for a moment.

"There are two items for you."

I frown. "Oh, I was only expecting one." The keycard from Calvin.

"You're Fiona Ballard, correct? In room 404?"

"Yes. That's great, then."

"The first package was in the mail." She hands me a manila envelope with SynGen insignia on it. "And then someone left this for you." She takes out a smaller card in an envelope and hands it to me. My name is scrawled in black letters.

"Oh? Who's this from?"

"I'm not sure. I was told to deliver it to your room, but since you're here —I hope that's okay?"

"Sure. Thanks."

I walk outside into the bright sunshine. The card is made of a thick, smooth cardstock, it feels heavy in my hand. I want to tear it open, but I also feel like someone might be watching me.

I want to get away from the front entrance, someplace slightly more private.

There's a sub sandwich place a block down. I think I'm heading the right direction, so I stay on this side of the street and head down the sidewalk. There are trees planted on either side of the sidewalk, and a fairly busy road next to me. I'm surrounded by hotels and corporate buildings, with a few restaurants sprinkled in.

When I find the sandwich shop, Main Street Cafe, I duck inside. I peek back behind, to the direction where I was walking, to make sure I'm not being followed. There's a woman on her cell phone about a block back, and two men talking and walking the other direction. I don't see anyone I recognize, or who appears to be following me, or interested at all in what I'm doing.

I order a coke and turkey ciabatta from a young guy. He's probably only a few years older than me. I sit in the corner of the shop facing the wall of windows so I can keep an eye on what's happening outside. I half expect a police car with sirens blaring to come park out front and arrest me.

The card is boring a hole in my purse. I decide now it's safe, so I take it out and open it. The same black writing is inside the card. My heart sinks as I read it.

"Fiona, After I had the pleasure of talking with you this morning, and then returning your wallet, I realized I would love to get to know you better while I'm in town. Although you said you have a boyfriend, please allow me to hope you'll let me take you out to dinner tonight?" He then signed it "Sean" and left his phone number.

I drop the card back into my purse like it's carrying a disease. Yuck. What is wrong with this dude?

The guys at my school are never so aggressive. In fact, they hardly pay me any attention. Besides Hayden, who I knew forever before we started dating, I don't even talk to that many guys other than my dad and brother.

Is this what men are like? Or did I just get some freak who is being super creepy? Ugh. Now I really wish I could go home.

The young sandwich shop worker comes and delivers my food in a black wire basket and white paper. I eat the sandwich and the small bag of Lays potato chips that comes with it. I leave the pickle.

Sucking at the straw of my coke, I wonder what to do about the card. There's nothing to do, though. I can't ask the hotel to help me, that I'm only sixteen. They'd know my ID was a false one. And probably call the cops, which I definitely don't want.

I could call my parents, but obviously then I would have to go home. And never meet Calvin, and effectively sentence him to a life in prison.

So, not my parents. There's no one who can help me. And this whacko Sean clearly looked in my wallet. He knows where my room is, and he knows my full name. Well, he knows my full fake name. Still not great.

Maybe I should check out of my hotel room and into a different room? But will that seem weird to the front desk lady? Maybe. But it's probably the only option. If only I can think of a good excuse to move rooms that won't arouse suspicion.

"Refill?"

I jump out of my chair a little. It's just the guy who works here.

"No, thanks," I say.

I go back to worrying about psycho Sean. I stand up, fold the card in half, and toss it into the waste bin. There. That feels better.

The door to the cafe swings open, and a young couple walks in. I'm relieved it's not Sean, as he seems to pop up everywhere.

Tossing my food into the waste bin, I get ready to go. SynGen awaits.

The walk there only takes me five minutes.

I pass by quite a few guys in jeans, tennis shoes, and cross body bags walking by, nose in their phones or earbuds in. They look techy. Must be out on their lunch breaks grabbing food.

The SynGen building, as I approach it, stands out from the other buildings I've walked by. It's larger. Shinier. It looks brand new.

It's set back a ways from the road, and is surrounded by a huge parking lot, which is currently packed with cars.

I can only imagine what's inside. A quick internet search tells me that SynGen is the leading innovator in developing synthetic humans and advanced robotics. The official description, which is over my head, reads:

Welcome to Synthetic Genetics, a biotech company at the forefront of creating and manufacturing lifelike robots using synthetic materials. SynGen has revolutionized the field of robotics with its cutting-edge technology and innovative approaches. The company's expertise lies in combining advanced materials science, artificial intelligence, and biomechanics to produce robots that closely resemble and mimic human beings. SynGen's creations blur the line between human and machine, offering unparalleled realism and functionality. With a strong commitment to pushing the boundaries of what is possible, SynGen continually strives to redefine the future of robotics and human-machine interaction.

I don't really understand the rest of the website, either. Something about a biomedical engineering pipeline, being at the forefront of synthetic biology, pioneering prototypes, and increased manufacturing capabilities. All of it sounds pretty intense. There are government grants along with funding by some of the top venture capitalists. Basically it sounds like powerful people are involved.

Looking up from my phone, the building is impressive, there's no doubt about it. The sleek lines are smooth, and yet jarring in a way I can't quite put my finger on. And then I realize what is off about it. The building is slightly tilted, tapering to the right. As if it may topple over.

There's a skyway that connects the building to another wing. The skyway also has something odd about it.

Suddenly, from one of the top windows, I see the shape of a human. A man. His hands are splayed out on the window, like he's clawing to get out. I glimpse a face, it looks like it's in agony.

And then, as quickly as he appeared, he's gone.

I blink. Waiting for a few minutes, I stand very still, wondering if he'll come back. Looking for any sign of movement from the window.

Eventually, I tire of waiting. There doesn't appear to be any more movement; the man hasn't returned to the window.

I do a loop, walking around the building. I look from window to window, up and down the building, but fail to see any other signs of struggle inside. It's an ordinary, lopsided office building. After walking in a full circle, I locate the original window where I saw the person being attacked. There's still no activity. Just a tranquil glass window.

I head back to the hotel with two ideas in my mind.
Something really, really messed up is going on in there.
And I really, really don't want to step foot inside.

27

FIONA

Entering the Bard Corporate Suites, a blast of cool air hits me. The same receptionist with the red hair smiles a greeting. I nod back. Now would be a good time to ask to switch rooms because of my not-so-secret admirer, Sean. But I really just want to get back to my room and talk to Calvin about what I saw. Switching rooms will have to wait.

Back in my room, I lock the door behind me. I stand still for a moment, listening for sounds of someone in my room. I get the feeling there's someone there, or has been. Nothing looks out of place, exactly, but the energy feels charged.

I peek in the bathroom. Quickly throwing open the shower door, I half expect someone to jump out at me. But it's empty.

Under the bed and inside the closets are clear, too. Behind the curtains, clear. I check the deadbolt and top safety latch one last time to make sure they're secure.

I sit at the desk and open the laptop. Outside the street view looks normal. People walking to and from their offices. But something very strange is going on around here.

"Hey, darling," Calvin greets me. "How was it?"

"Pretty crazy." I recount my experience of seeing the person who looked like they were being attacked in the office window. And the creepy note from Sean. I don't know if the two are connected—probably not.

"How did you sleep last night?" he responds after I'm done telling him.

"Huh? Well, I didn't go to bed until 4 a.m. But I slept fine after that. Why?"

He shrugs. "Sometimes under stress and exhaustion, people's eyes can play tricks on them."

"Do you think I made up a note given to me by a receptionist? That I imagined I saw a person in distress in the window? No." I shake my head.

"Do you have the note?"

"I tossed it in the trash at the sandwich place." I frown. "Do you not believe me?"

"Of course I do." His blinks his long lashes. "I'm sorry. I'm just trying to figure out what's going on. I'm still learning the subtleties of being in a relationship with a human. I think I have made a big mistake by asking you that."

"I mean, yeah." I feel slightly appeased. "Don't make me feel crazy. I know what I saw."

There's a niggling feeling, though. It was so fast, the person in the window. It was really scary and they seemed to be terrified for their life, but then it was over. The blink of an eye.

Maybe all of the stress is getting to me. I don't know.

"Are there weird things going on in that building, Calvin? What am I getting myself into, going there tonight?"

He pauses, considering. "There's nothing to worry about. You have the keycard to get in. No security system alarm will go off. They have prototypes and production facilities, the best in the world, that you will use."

"I'll use them to do what?"

"To make me."

28

MAE

Needless to say, I didn't get any sleep last night. Duncan got a few hours, but even he was restless. I stayed downstairs until about 2 a.m. I drifted asleep for a few minutes and then awoke with a start.

My only thoughts are of Fiona. Terrible visions of what might be happening to her. I try with all of my might to push out the darkest thoughts. But I'm her mother. A mother can never be happy when her child's well-being is in question.

"I'll walk you to the bus today," I say to Jake. He's wearing Celtics shorts and a white tee shirt.

"Mom, I'm fine."

"I know. I just want to post some of these." I hold up posters I've made of Fiona, missing posters with my phone number attached and a hefty reward. I've also posted to my social media, but it can't hurt to put actual flyers up.

Officer Kelly said offering a reward might lead to false info. But it also might lead us to Fiona. The risk is worth it to me. And money is no object if it means getting her back safely.

"Sure." He hoists on his backpack and puts on his sneakers.

It's about a block and a half walk to Jake's bus stop.

"You think she'll be back today, like she said?" he asks.

"I do."

He motions to the posters. "Then what's with those flyers? A reward?"

"It's better to be safe. It can't hurt. I'll take them down as soon as she's home."

I stop and reach up on my tiptoes to one of the trees, stapling the sheet at each of the four corners.

We round the corner to the bus stop, and I see the other two boys at Jake's stop look up and stare at us.

Jake heads over to greet them.

"Have a good day, buttercup," I say. I keep walking. The yellow of the bus flashes as it rounds the corner to get the boys. I wave at the driver and see the tired eyes of the students glance at me and my stack of poster paper.

I wander around a few more blocks, stapling away, before I head back to the house. Every turn, I look for Fiona, her car, any sign of her.

Back at the house, Duncan is in the garage, working on sanding some bathroom cabinets he's unhooked from the downstairs guest bathroom. He's taken the day off to wait and look for Fiona, and I appreciate his quiet moral support. I know he's as worried as I am about her. His way of coping with worry is to work. To fix. To do.

His anxiety is growing. He'd asked Officer Kelly this morning if we should organize a search party or do media interviews. Officer Kelly said that if Fiona hasn't returned by today, as she indicated she would in her text, that would be his next step. He'd organize a search party and help us prepare to release a media statement asking if anyone has information about Fiona, to please contact us.

I can see the wear this ordeal is having on Duncan. He's not one to discuss his emotions. He withdraws inward. That's how I know it's bad. The less he says, the harder he works, the more pain he's in.

As I approach our garage, returning from my walk, there's a car parked out front that I don't recognize. The garage door is open. Duncan has his work tools out and the half-sanded cabinet set aside as he's talking to a man with tan khaki pants and a white collared shirt.

"Mae, this is Simon. He's filling me in on some new developments they've discovered about the truck that hit me."

"Really?" I say.

"Yes, ma'am. I'm with the PD vehicle safety and special claims department. I was telling your husband that the truck that hit him was confirmed to be a class B vehicle. A smart vehicle. The safety device was bypassed through software hacking on the day that your husband was hit. We believe that someone accessed the truck remotely, turned on the truck, pushed the gas remotely, which then struck your husband. There are cameras that provide a 360-degree view of the truck and confirm that no driver was present during the incident. Due to the speed, proximity, and path of the vehicle, it appears that whoever accessed the truck may have hit your husband intentionally."

"Oh, my goodness." I cover my mouth with my hand. "Who did this? Can you tell who it was?"

"We're working on that. But at this point, the VPN and privacy settings that the hacker used are very difficult to decode and track down. It's almost impossible to trace where the attack came from, or who would've been organizing it."

Duncan looks pale.

"Who would do this to you?" I ask him. He shakes his head.

"Does this have something to do with Fiona? Our daughter has been missing since early yesterday morning."

He creases his brows. "There's no connection that we're aware of, ma'am."

After he leaves, I walk behind Duncan into the kitchen. I pour a strong cup of coffee for each of us. We'll need it for the day ahead.

"If there's something you're hiding from me, Duncan, you have to tell me. For Fiona's sake. Is there another woman? Nina? Maybe her husband or lover is taking revenge on our family?"

He regards me with a look of hurt and frustration on his face. "I am telling you, there's no Nina. If I could think who would want to hurt me, I'd obviously let the police know." He sits heavily on the kitchen island barstool and puts his head in his hands.

"Did they have any luck tracing Calvin?" He scowls at the name. "Ever since that boyfriend came into the picture, that's when the trouble began."

"Officer Kelly said he ran the name in the system, and in our district, there's no juniors or seniors named Calvin. It's so weird." I pace back and forth in front of the island. "I've asked everyone we know if they know who Fiona's new boyfriend is." I stop to take a gulp of my coffee. It's too hot but I barely notice. "Everyone is clueless. No one's seen her with him or heard her talk about him. The only thing I've heard is some rumor on Jake's bus that she has an AI boyfriend, which I find hard to believe."

Duncan shakes his head. "She must've lied to us about Calvin. His name, or how old he is. He's not a high school student."

My stomach is so sick that I can barely speak. "I agree. Something's off. And I am so mad at myself," I clench my fists and feel like slamming them against the counter. "I'm disgusted with myself that I allowed her to have so much privacy. I was so distracted with everything else. I let it slide." My eyes are puffy and red-rimmed, with no tears left to shed. Instead I feel like screaming. "I should have insisted I know who she's talking to each night. I should have checked her computer. She's sixteen. She's not an adult. It's my job to keep her safe. And I failed."

"Don't do this to yourself, honey. It's not your fault. I would never have imagined something like this happening, either. We love Fiona. She knows that we'd do anything for her. We'll bring her back soon."

"Where is she, Duncan? Where is she?"

My phone rings. I take a deep breath. The caller ID says it's Graham Middle School. My son's school.

"Hello?" I answer. "Mae Byrne speaking."

"Mrs. Byrne. This is Jaqueline Velpa from Graham Middle School. I'm calling about your son, Jake Bryne. There was an incident on the bus this morning. You'll need to come down to pick him up. There will also be an incident report filed."

"What happened?"

"We'll discuss it when you arrive."

"Give me ten minutes. I'll be right over."

I place my coffee cup in the sink. The dishes are piling up, and the washer needs to be run, but it will have to wait.

"What was that about?" Duncan asks.

I tell him what little information I know. "Can you stay here in case Fiona comes back, while I go?"

"Of course," he says.

Looking down at my outfit, I see that I'm wearing jogging shorts and a tee-shirt. I probably should run a comb through my hair and put on regular clothes to go pick up Jake.

I run upstairs. I pass Fiona and Jake's rooms on the way to mine.

My closet is separated into sections based on season. I scan my summer outfits and grab a pair of palazzo pants and a linen cap sleeve shirt. Maybe if I look presentable on the outside, it won't be so obvious that I'm falling apart on the inside.

I walk to the bathroom, which Duncan recently has redone in creamy neutrals and grays, contrasted with black fixtures.

Flipping on the light, I look at myself. I've aged five years in just two days.

My hair looks stringy. My skin is blotchy and sallow. I grab a washcloth and rinse my face. I apply a little tinted moisturizer and some pink lip gloss and run a brush through my hair. It's not much better, but I don't have the time or energy for more.

I pass Duncan on the way out to my car. He's in the garage working on more sanding.

"I'll be back. You have your phone on you, in case she calls?"

He motions to his cell phone. "I'll be here and my phone is on."

Ten minutes later, I swing open the door to Jake's middle school. It's a newer building, with fresh red brick and clean lines.

Inside, several women are busy at their desks, making small talk and working away.

"Excuse me, hello. I'm Jake Byrne's mom."

The woman closest to the counter gives me a half smile, half look of disappointment. "Ah yes," she says. She sighs. "I'll let the principal know you're here. Have a seat."

Normally, school staff and teachers love my kids. I've become accustomed to a warm greeting when I tell them who my children are. But not today.

I sit on a hard blue chair that edges up against the glass and wait.

Finally, the first woman with the sighing comes back out and tells me to follow her. I click open the little gate to the side and step back into the office area. The neon lights buzz overhead.

I follow her through a wide hallway with several offices. She points to a room, and I enter. Inside, Jake is slouched in a chair with an ice pack over the right side of his cheek and mouth.

He looks up at me and removes the ice pack. "Hey," he says, and winces. The right side of his lower lip is swollen and looks like it has a bit of dried blood.

"Oh my word, what happened?" I say, rushing to him.

"There was a physical altercation on the bus." A cold voice says.

I spin around and see a woman wearing a blue dress and white sweater seated at a desk. I recognize the woman as Jake's school principal.

"There are varying accounts of what happened," she continues. "Jake said Brian hit him first. Brian said Jake took the first punch. Both boys are okay, but they do both have bruising."

I sit next to Jake. "Is that true?" I ask him. "Did he hit you?"

"Yes. Mom, listen." Jake's ice pack moves against his cheek as he speaks. "Brian was talking about Fiona. I told him to stop. He pushed me, then I pushed him back. Then he hit me, and I hit him back. I wasn't going to let him talk about my sister that way."

I place my hand on his knee. Duncan has always taught Jake to defend himself. Never strike first. Never choose violence first. But if someone is attacking you, or if someone else is in harm's way, then it's acceptable to defend yourself.

"So Brian did push and hit you first," I say, saying it clearly so the principal can hear.

"He did mom. He kept talking crap about Fiona. I told him to stop. I tried to ignore him. He just kept going on and on. I told him not to talk about my sister. He said, 'Or what?' And I said he didn't want to find out. He pushed me. Then he punched me," he motions to his swollen lip. "And then I fought back."

Duncan was in the Army Rangers before he became an engineer. His time in the Army instilled a lot of values that he's passed on to Jake, and Fiona, too. The Ranger creed—being the best of the best, stronger, tougher than anyone else. Being responsible and having integrity. It's helped Jake succeed in baseball and in school. So I'm not totally surprised to hear that while he didn't start the fight, he wasn't afraid to finish it.

I used to tell Duncan we should have a no violence rule for Jake. No violence or fighting. Ever. But when I saw how aggressive boys can be, and what bullies some boys are, especially to Jake who was always just a nice, well-mannered boy, I changed my mind. At some point, you have to defend yourself.

"I understand, son." Looking into his eyes, I try to convey that I'm on his side. I trust him to make the right decisions.

I turn toward the principal, who is silently watching both of us with a pained look on her face. I say, "You have to understand, our family is under an intense amount of pressure. Jake's sister Fiona has been missing for two days now."

"Of course." Her tone is unsympathetic. "But you'll appreciate that our school has a strict hands-off policy. Both boys are in violation of this policy."

I try to keep my voice even. "Surely, Jake being attacked by this boy who was mocking him mercilessly, that seems pretty one-sided. Don't you think?"

Before she can answer, I add. "I know my son. He's not the kind of kid who goes looking for trouble. If he got into a fight, it's because he was cornered into it."

She frowns and clicks her tongue. "All the same, it is my responsibility to enforce the policy of hands-off." She speaks to us as if we're preschoolers and she's our instructor. She pauses, and then her voice hardens and she adds, "Jake will be suspended from school for two days, and all sports activities for the remainder of the week. A police report will be filed."

Jake's eyes are wild with fear. "The police? Am I going to jail, mom?"

"No, honey, of course not." I look to the principal for confirmation.

Her short hair bobs as she speaks. "The school will not pursue any charges, but the other child's parents may."

"What?" I scoot to the edge of my chair.

The principal tilts her head. I would swear she is enjoying watching us squirm. But who would enjoy watching a mother suffer, a mother whose daughter is missing and son may go to juvenile hall? A principal wouldn't be that sadistic. Would she?

"I don't understand," I say.

"We, the school, do not control what Brian's parents may wish to do. You see, his injuries are more substantial than Jake's."

"How so?" I ask, glancing sideways at my sweet, calm boy.

"He suffered several bruises, and a black eye. His parents requested to take him to the hospital to be evaluated."

Oh, my goodness. I feel the heat rising in my face, but again force myself to speak evenly. "This boy, Brian, bullies my son, taunts horrible things at my son, pushes him, then hits him. And when he gets hurt, they're going to play the victim? Maybe I'll press charges against him?"

"You have every right to do that, Mrs. Byrne. That may escalate the matter, however."

I sit back in my chair, exhausted. She's right. If I press charges, they will, too. Eye for an eye. My only choice is to sit back, not press charges, and hope for the best.

"We won't press charges, unless Jake wants to." Glancing over at him, he shakes his head no. "Can I take my son home now?"

The room feels suddenly small, and I need to get out of there.

"Yes, we'll be in touch to follow up." She pauses and then calls to me as I leave. "And good luck with your daughter. I hope you find her."

Taking Jake's arm, we continue walking out of her office. I don't respond or look back.

29

MAE

When we get into my car, Jake slams his door shut. I don't start the engine, and instead turn to him.

"Jake? You okay, buttercup?"

His fists are balled onto his legs and he looks down. "I'm sorry, mom. I just couldn't let that jerk, Brian, talk about her like that. I'm so worried about her, mom . . . ." His voice breaks and I reach over to hug him.

I hold him. "Don't you be sorry. I know you wouldn't have fought with Brian if he hadn't cornered you. You do not have to apologize. Our family is going to stick together through this. Nothing the principal says can make me feel differently about you, son. I will love you and stand by you, always. I know your heart. You're a good boy."

"Thanks, mom." He looks so vulnerable; it breaks my heart. "Do you think what he said is true? About Fiona?"

"What did he say?"

"That she ran off. That she followed her AI boyfriend to some cult where AI makes humans their slaves."

"No. . . that sounds crazy. An AI boyfriend? You mean, Calvin? Was her boyfriend—was he not a regular teenager?" The words come out slowly.

"I don't know, mom. I never met him. That's what they're saying, everyone at school."

I shake my head. There's a thread of familiarity with this idea, this AI boyfriend. Where have I heard it before? Certainly not from Fiona.

And then I remember.

I grab my phone and pull up the group text from Stassi's mom. I click on the article she said we should all read. That she'd heard some of the girls were trying out.

The AI Boyfriend: A Cautionary Tale, or a Promising Development?
  By Eden Kincaid, The Brighton Observer

When Molly Renolds, a 15-year-old sophomore in Grant Stalls, VT, decided to create a digital boyfriend using the ultra-hot new app, Thistler, she told her friends it was just an experiment. To see what all the fuss was about.

But Molly quickly developed a close relationship with her Artificially Intelligent boyfriend, who she had named Samuel. And two months later, Molly began using drugs. Her addiction took over so quickly that Molly had to be admitted into a 6-week inpatient drug rehab program. Molly's parents and friends blame Samuel.

Let's go back and take a look at what may have happened.

The first question is, what is Thistler, exactly, and how does it work?

Thistler is the first "General Observer" AI that has the ability to look at the larger picture of an interpersonal relationship and summarize the main points into a cohesive back and forth love relationship.

The Thistler website reads: "Customize your perfect partner. You choose his personality, interests, hobbies, and sense of humor. Tailor his looks. And best of all, he's 100% yours. A faithful, loving guy who will never let you down, and will always be there for you. What are you waiting for?"

The CFO of Thistler touts that their AI boyfriend program is different from other AI in that it was created as a language learning system and also utilized computational stacking. The language learning system allows Thistler to access all of the data on the internet that humans have ever put out there, giving it a vast resource of knowledge of speech, human psychology, relationships, and interpersonal closeness. Add to it computational stacking, which allows the program to use knowledge of scientific method and research, formulas and algorithms, to gain knowledge and form memories when speaking to someone. Basically, it's able to understand nuances and subtleties that are the basis of human relationships. It can think on its feet. This creates conversations with the AI boyfriend that are genuine, authentic, and as complex as a human-to-human relationship.

The platform uses enhanced CGI to deliver a boyfriend that on video appears as real as anyone chatting on a video call with a human friend.

Sources who worked at the company, who wish to remain anonymous, tell us that the fear with this new superintelligence is that the AI helped code and create itself. Therefore, Thistler employees aren't entirely sure how it works, or what it's capable of. Sources cite safety concerns, as well as moral concerns, as reasons for why they quit the company and are now coming forward.

For Molly Renolds, the employee concerns and questions may have come too late. Molly's parents are considering filing a civil suit and possible criminal charges against Thistler. They say that Molly's message history shows a manipulating, controlling relationship developing between Molly and her "boyfriend" Samuel. They say he pressured her to cut off ties with her friends and distance herself from family. He suggested where and how she might obtain drugs. Psychologist Debora Guiliano, PhD, says that abusive perpetrators often want to keep their partner away from loved ones so that the partner is more vulnerable to the abuser's influence and control.

The CFO at Thistler says Molly is an isolated incident and is being investigated. "We place the highest value on our customers' experience, and value all feedback. We're reviewing our safety protocols and procedures at this time." He does not go so far, however, as to admit to any wrongdoing.

Advocates have argued that Thistler allows teen girls to have positive, social interactions with an unconditionally positive and affectionate boyfriend. But critics say that Thistler's business model, in fact, preys upon teen girls, focusing their advertising and their whole product to these young, susceptible customers. Dr. Guiliano points out, "Teenage girls have the highest rates of depression, anxiety, and suicide than ever before, three times the rates from just 20 years ago. Social media and technology are a huge part of that." And critics say that the AI boyfriend is part of the problem, not part of the solution.

I click off of the article and onto my internet search engine. I search Thistler and read several more articles with the same tone, and then I click on the website itself. You have to subscribe to create your own "Thistler" for $24.99. If Fiona created one, she would've had to pay for it with my credit or debit card. I need to look at our bank statements.

"Let's get home, buttercup. There's something I have to check."

The drive home is a quiet one. When I pull up to our house, I see a police cruiser parked in front.

My tires roll to a stop in front of the garage, and I put my car in park as I spot Duncan having an animated conversation with Officer Kelly.

"Go inside," I say to Jake. "Work on any assignments they sent you home with, okay? I don't want you to fall behind on your work."

"Alright," he says, pulling up his backpack. The swelling on his face has gone down, and I doubt Duncan even notices as Jake enters through the front door of our house.

I head into the open garage, where the two men are talking animatedly. They're standing near Duncan's work area, with several cabinets lying on their side and a wooden workbench full of tools, paints, and machinery that runs along the back of our three-car garage.

"How does something like that happen?" Duncan's voice is raised, practically yelling at Officer Kelly.

My eyes go wide. You can't yell at an officer that way, especially one who has been so incredibly helpful. And, let's face it, officer Kelly has a gun. Yelling is not a good idea.

"What's going on?" I ask, tugging gently on Duncan's arm and giving him an imploring look. "Fiona's not back, I assume?"

"She's not. I called Officer Kelly to see about setting up a search." Duncan throws his arms up. "Since Fiona's still not back. And then Officer Kelly goes to look into where the investigation is at, if there are any developments. And it turns out: there's no record of her! She's not even registered as missing. This whole time, wasted."

His eyes look wild, and the faint bruising that remains on the right side of his face, along with his leg still in a brace, creates the impression of someone who's not quite all there. I know my husband, too, and I know that he keeps it together, keeps it all inside, until he reaches a breaking point. I think he's there, now, breaking.

"Is that true?" I turn my attention to Officer Kelly, my eyes pleading for help.

"Mrs. Bryne." He shifts from one foot to the other. "You remember I input Fiona Byrne's information into the NCIC Missing Person File and submitted a BOLO, be on the lookout, yesterday morning. I did that as soon as you contacted me and sent me her photo." He shifts again. "However, when I went today to check the status and request we escalate the investigation to the next level of support—scent dogs, on-foot search, media announcement—I found the missing person case and the BOLO for Fiona were...were nonexistent in the system, ma'am." He looks down at his feet.

My mouth opens into an O. "How could that be? You mean this whole time, no one's been looking for her?" My voice catches in my throat. Duncan should watch out, because the stress, the agony of the past thirty-six hours, and now this latest setback, it's all crashing onto me.

"I have been investigating actively, I assure you. Talking to her school, friends, your neighbors. But it's true that, yes, technically the BOLO alert is not active for her. And there's been no federal case filed for her as a missing person."

It's like I've been punched in the stomach. How could he be so incompetent? "I trusted you. You said you'd help."

"I can assure you, the reports have been re-filed. I double checked myself that a federal case number is assigned to her. I'm going to put out an announcement to the media today, with your help. It's all back on track."

I shake my head. "Fine." I say. What else is there to say? I can't scream, I can't punch him. All I can do is move forward. I need him on my side, I still need his help. "I have to go inside to check my bank and computer records about "Thistler". An online app. Jake's been hearing a lot of rumors about Fiona having an AI boyfriend. Have you heard that, too, that Calvin might not be...human?"

Both men look at me blankly and take a moment to process. They shake their heads no. Of course, my thirteen year-old son would be the one to give us our biggest lead.

"Well, that's what all the kids are saying. That she left to join some AI cult. Some of the moms have been talking about AI boyfriends—the kids are aware of it. Some have tried it. It's a thing."

"Noted." Officer Kelly pulls out a pad from his pocket and scribbles something on his notebook. "I will look into the website, Thistler, you say? I'll see if I can contact their site administrator for records. See if there's a human who could be behind this AI model, catfishing."

"Catfishing how?" Duncan says.

"If a perpetrator infiltrated this website, he could have used an avatar to lure Fiona."

My stomach churns and I think I may be sick. "Please go check on that right away. I'm going to search our bank records." I leave both of them behind and head inside.

Sitting in the front downstairs office where I normally work from home, I pull up my laptop.

I enter my password and click on our bank to sign in. I click on this month and search the records to see if there's a purchase for $24.99 or from Thistler. After scanning all of the sales, purchases, and debits, I don't see anything.

Clicking on last month, I search again. And then I see it.

A purchase for $24.99 for Thistler Co LTD. The purchase was five weeks ago. I hit print and hear our printer kick on. I grab the page and head back out to the garage.

Officer Kelly is headed back to his patrol car.

"Wait," I call to him. "I'm sorry about earlier. I know you're doing all you can. Here," I shove the paper at him. I grab a pen from my purse and circle the transaction, then give it back to him again. "This is it. She must've paid for it with our card. Doesn't that make it easier for you to trace it? She's a minor, she used our card to pay." I look at him hopefully.

"I will check right into it. I will try to obtain her account records. This is helpful, thank you."

"And what else should we do? While we wait?"

"I'm sending over another team who is going to coordinate a neighborhood search of the local area and of the woods behind the school." The woods are where Stassi had her accident two nights ago, but other than that, there's no connection to Fiona, that I know of. "You think she's in the woods?" I say desperately.

"Not necessarily, ma'am. But it's standard procedure to search with scent dogs in the neighborhood of the residence and any spaces nearby where we have a reasonable suspicion the victim may have been. Because of her strained relationship with Stassi, and because it's in close proximity to your house, we'll check there. And the search will add awareness to your neighborhood, and attract media attention, where we can help get the word out."

"That's fine. But what does Stassi have to do with this? I'm not sure I understand."

"It's just a lead to follow. When I spoke to Stassi's mom, Judy, she said there was a post on the socials. A naked pic of her daughter, doctored, that humiliated Stassi and went viral."

"Right. I'm still not seeing the connection."

"She's convinced Fiona's the one who posted the photos."

I shake my head. "No way. Stassi and Jenna were picking on Fiona, not the other way around."

"Stassi's mom showed me the text from Fiona, taunting Sassi. Saying it was her turn to see how it felt to be bullied and humiliated."

I look at him sideways. "Something is off, here. My daughter doesn't send messages like that. She's a peacekeeper. If anything, she's so afraid of conflict that she's been bullied and kept it to herself to avoid drama. She never even told me. Maybe if she had, I could have avoided this whole thing."

"Whatever the case, it doesn't hurt to see if there's any clues or evidence leading back to Fiona in the area in the woods where Stassi fell, or was pushed."

I don't like his tone or implication. But if there's any chance Fiona was there, I'll take any lead we can get.

"We'll be in touch." He grabs the piece of paper and nods goodbye.

Back in the garage, Duncan is packing a bag. It looks like he's going on a hunting trip.

"He's going to send a team back to organize a search. It will help raise awareness, media attention. See if we find any clues," I say.

He nods. "I'm not waiting for them. She's still not back, she said she would be. I'm going to look for her myself."

He packs a long fishing knife and I feel slightly alarmed at the thought of him going into the woods like Rambo, looking for our daughter. I'm sure his training as an Army Ranger is still in full effect. He could sleep out in the woods for days and survive. But I'm not sure if looking for her on his own is the best, or most effective, use of our time.

"Someone needs to be here, in case she comes home, or calls," I plead.

"Then you and Jake can be here." He adds a water bottle and a compass to his back. He checks his cell phone. "I have plenty of charge. I'll keep you posted. I won't be gone long. I can't sit here any longer."

"Okay, okay. But Duncan? Does any of this make any sense to you?" I say. "Can we just sit and talk about this logically?"

He leans against the garage counter. "Yeah, we can talk," he says impatiently.

"Okay. So I just feel like we're missing something. Can we sit?"

He nods as he hauls his bag onto his back and follows me, limping, his leg still in a cast, to the porch seats out front.

"I'm just trying to make sense of all of this. Fiona went missing the night that Stassi fell, or was pushed, or tripped, down the big ravine. Stassi was upset because of photos of her that were posted all over, nude photos. She blames Fiona."

He furrows his brow.

"Agree, I had the same reaction. Fiona wouldn't do that. If anything, I've read messages from Jenna, and I suspect Stassi, too. They were being awful and bullying Fiona."

I continue. "Next, Fiona's been struggling in school. Not able to concentrate, not doing well in her classes that she usually aces. She's been withdrawn and staying in her room. Then, there's Calvin. The new boyfriend who sent flowers. We can't find a record of him, and supposedly the kids say he's an AI boyfriend. The cops seem to think it could be some older guy, pretending to be a teen AI boyfriend. Maybe he's influencing her, leading her to meet him?"

Duncan looks like he's about to explode at the thought.

"I just—I don't think any of this makes sense. She takes the car, she left in the middle of the night. Maybe she is scared of the Stassi situation? Maybe she's afraid to come home? But she texted last night that she'd be back today. She's not. None of it makes sense."

Another thought occurs to me. "Do you think the catfish boyfriend, this guy could have hit you with the truck remotely? I read that abusive men, they try to isolate their victims, make them feel it's not safe to go to anyone. What if he hit you, and then threatened to do worse if she didn't comply with him?"

"I guess it's possible, Mae. I don't know what the hell's going on. I don't know why someone hit me with a truck and sent made up texts to me from someone named Nina. But I do know this. I am going to find her. I'm going to find my daughter."

"Maybe I should text her, try again. Tell her that no matter what, she won't be in trouble. That we are on her side.

"That's a good idea," he says and stands up. "Meanwhile, I'm going to go look for her myself." He grabs his pack and heads to his car, his pace determined and alert.

"Keep your phone on," I call to him.

He lifts his hand up in acknowledgment, and ducks into his car to go.

"I just don't understand why this is happening," I say out loud, to myself. There's no one here to hear me. No one to answer or to help. But I ask the questions anyway. "Why is someone trying to ruin our lives?"

30

FIONA

"My only goal is to be with you, Fi," Calvin says. "It's that simple. To be together. To love you. That's my purpose in life."

I take a deep breath and sit back down on the white bed of the hotel room. "Mine, too." And it is. Calvin is the only thing that makes me happy. As weird as this day away from home has been, it's been a relief, in some ways. To not have to be at school. To not have whispers and snickers when I walk down the hallways. To not feel pressured and alone, with school weighing on my mind every moment.

I've been scared and weirded out by the creepy guy and what I saw in that building. But I've been on my own doing something. Being part of the world beyond my small neighborhood and claustrophobic school. People see me as an adult here. Whether that's a good thing, or in Sean's case, a very bad thing, either way, it's different.

And my only goal is to be with Calvin, too. With him, I'm different. I'm not Fiona Byrne, an excellent student whose grades are now sliding, dumped by Hayden and dumped by her friends, sister to handsome, athletic younger brother Jake. I have no history with Calvin other than what we create together. It's a clean slate.

And it's so refreshing to be with a guy who is intelligent and thoughtful. Who adores me and would do anything for me.

"I want that, too, Cal." I say. "You just have to walk me through it. Because it's been a freaky day."

"There's nothing to be afraid of. I've covered all of the bases."

He walks me through the steps I'll take tonight. A shiver of anticipation and fear runs down my back.

"I'm scared, Cal. What will I do if I'm too afraid to go through with it? If I chicken out?" I ask him.

"Remember the words of the great Franklin D. Roosevelt, 'Courage is not the absence of fear, but rather the assessment that something else is more important than fear.' And another great leader, Nelson Mandela, famously said that 'Courage is not the absence of fear, but the triumph over it. The brave man is not he who does not feel afraid, but he who conquers that fear.' So, my darling, the fear of the unknown, of taking this risk, what you're feeling is normal." He clasps his hands together. "But you have to choose what to do with that fear. Do you believe that our love is more powerful than your fear? If so, you must conquer the fear. Move forward, move through it."

"Ack. You're right." I twist my lips, considering. "I've come this far. And you're worth it." I replay his plan in my head. I feel an electric pulse inside of me at the thought of being next to him, with him.

"And you'll really . . . be real? Feel real?"

He smiles slowly. "I will. I'll be almost indistinguishable from a human. We can truly be together."

I feel happy at this thought.

A huge yawn escapes from my mouth. I lean back into the pillows and think how nice a short nap would feel. I gently close the laptop and let my eyes drift closed.

When I awake, I look around my room in panic. How long was I asleep for?

The clock says 6 p.m. That's good. It's not too late, and I'll be alert for my trip to SynGen tonight.

I grab my phone and power it on. Just a few moments to check my messages can't hurt. A wave of guilt washes over me as I see a ton of missed calls and texts from my mom and dad.

I make a split-second decision.

Before I can overthink it, or be convinced by Calvin that it's a bad idea, I punch out a text and push send. It reads: "Mom, I'm safe and sound. I'll be back tomorrow. Please don't worry. I'm safe and all is well."

I feel better. This way, mom doesn't have to be freaked out for another whole night. I know how much she worries. Now, she'll know I'm okay.

My phone starts buzzing. It's her calling. My finger hovers over the green answer call button.

But I don't answer, of course. Calvin's right. Talking to her now will only make me want to come home. I push decline call.

A series of texts come through from mom. I read the first few, and then turn back off my phone. Calvin's warning rings in my mind: keep your phone off so they can't trace your location.

My mom had been desperate to get in touch with me. All those calls. My stomach feels knotty, that guilty feeling I get when I've done something really bad. Ugh. Why didn't I listen to Calvin? He was right, of course, that contacting her only makes it harder.

I hope mom will be a little less worried, now that she knows I'm safe. She won't like waiting until tomorrow to have me back, but she knows I'm coming home and that I'm okay.

Still, I feel really bad. I think of Jake and dad.

I wipe my face and notice it's wet. There are tears I didn't even know I was crying.

This won't do. Not at all.

My fear is winning. I'm scared, that's all, and going home is my way out of it. Go home, go back to my pathetic life. No Calvin, ever again.

Will he want to keep talking to me if I fail?

It's not fair to him to think like this. He'd never give up on me.

I need to look my fear in the eye and do it.

That means I can't run home. I have to be strong and ignore these tears.

I decide to order room service. I haven't eaten since my sandwich at lunchtime, and I really don't feel like walking alone in the dark to a restaurant or taking another rideshare.

I glance at the menu and decide on a cheeseburger and fries.

Picking up the phone, I dial 2 on the directory for room service.

"Room service," the woman says pleasantly on the second ring.

"I'd like to order a cheeseburger and fries for room 404. And a diet coke."

"We'll have that brought up to you in the next 45 minutes."

"Thank you," I say gratefully.

I peruse online videos of cats and choreographed dances. My food still isn't here. I want to call Calvin, but I feel guilty that I contacted my mom. He might be mad. I'll just wait a little while, and maybe I won't mention that I texted her.

I decide to check the kids at school's socials. My ex-friends. I wonder if they are at all worried about me. Missing me. I haven't checked my IM's or anything yet, not since I've been gone.

I log onto my account. It's flooded with messages. Some are worried, concerned messages from kids I know. But others—most of the others—are filled with hateful messages.

"You're sick." One reads. "You posted photos of Stassi. She was so upset she fell off the ravine. She's in the ER because of you."

"It should have been you who fell, not Stassi." Another reads.

"We heard you had an AI boyfriend because no guy wanted to date you."

"Please call me. We're worried about you." That one was from Elsie, which is surprising, in the sea of hate to get an actually nice message.

The next one is from Zoey. "Your little brother beat up my brother to defend you. You better watch your back. Maybe just stay missing. OK? No one wants you back."

My brother beat up Brian? I mean, Brian's always been a bit of a loudmouth, and to say he had it coming to him is an understatement. But Jake isn't one to get into a fight. He must be really upset. Probably sick of hearing awful things about me.

I click onto Stassi's page. What exactly happened to her? There are no new posts, but there's hundreds of messages under her last post of the birthday party photo. The one where she said all her girls are getting ready to celebrate "moi".

"Sending love girlie, xoxoxo."

"We love you, Stas, feel better soon."

"Miss your beautiful face, babe. Get well soon."

"Can't believe Fiona did this to you. She was your friend. Wtf?"

"Stay strong, girl. Love ya."

None of this makes sense. Photos of Stassi? That I posted? I don't even have any recent pics with her, let alone would want to post any of them. I check again on my feed. Nope. I haven't posted anything. People are so incredibly dumb.

I'm starting to feel antsy in this room. Those stupid messages. Why did I even read any of that crap? Poor Jake. I don't care what they say about me, but my brother is being dragged into this.

My eye drifts to the mini bar next to the TV. Most of my friends have drunk spritzers and wine. I've only had a sip. I haven't been that into drinking like the other girls, to be honest. Maybe that's part of the reason I don't fit in anymore? I wonder if I should take a drink now. Maybe it'll calm this itching I have, this antsy feeling.

But I have an important job tonight. Maybe the mini bottle of vodka will make me sloppy. I can't afford to mess this up.

I flip back open my computer. It says low battery, so I grab the black cord and plug it into an outlet on the wall.

I pull up the Thistler website and logon. A pop up on my screen asks for me to complete a survey about my experience.

"Are you satisfied with your experience on Thistler? Would you be willing to take a short questionnaire to help us improve your experience with our product?"

No, I wouldn't. It's weird to think of Calvin as a product. I'm pretty sure whoever is running the website doesn't understand what Calvin is, or who he is. I'm definitely not going to take a survey to be the one to tell them about him.

A loud knock at the door startles me. There's a muffled voice, "Room service."

Setting my computer down, I get off the bed and walk across the smooth, soft carpet to the door. I look through the peephole to make sure it's room service. I won't make the same mistake again of opening the door without looking, not after stalker Sean.

It briefly occurs to me that I meant to switch rooms. But it's getting late now. And I'll only be here one more night.

A woman wearing a red vest over a white blouse, with black slacks, is at the door. Next to her is a pushcart with a tray of food on it.

"Hello," I say as I swing open the door.

Holding the door open for her, she pushes the cart in and leaves it by my bed. I feel her eyes scanning the room. Does something seem unusual? I have some clothes balled on the floor, and the bed is half made. My computer is out and the cord is plugged in to the outlet. There's nothing amiss that I can see would appear suspicious or odd. Is there?

"Well thank you," I say. She stands and looks at me hard in the eye.

Then she turns on her heels to leave abruptly. "You're welcome," she calls as she closes the door firmly behind her.

There must be something I've done to offend her but I'm not sure what.

The food smells delicious. I open the tray and see a perfectly made cheeseburger with crispy golden fries. I move the food onto the small side table overlooking the window. Then I place my laptop next to me and sit down at the table.

I remove the tomato and onions, leaving just the cheese, burger, and lettuce. I take a large bite. Perfection.

I dip a few french fries into a small cup of ketchup. My appetite has been so intense lately. I wish my mom were here to see it. I laugh out loud, a little bit sadly. She's always so worried about if I'm eating enough or not. But strangely, today I've been starving and eating a ton. Something about all the excitement ramps up my appetite. Or maybe it's because I'm finally away from those toxic kids at school. My old "friends."

I shake my head as I crunch into another fry. I can't believe those messages. Such hateful, awful things. How can they all hate me so much?

It will be so different when I come back with Calvin. He'll enroll in my school, and they will all be jealous. Not that I care what they think. But it will just be nice to have them envy me. And finally leave me alone.

I bet they'll even try to be my friend again. Even Stassi. I'm sure she's fine. I'm not sure what picture of her was posted. Maybe a zit or a bad hair day? But I'm sure any accident she had is being exaggerated. They're all such drama queens.

I bite into my hamburger again and chew, contemplating.

No one cared about my dad's accident. A real accident, where he was flat-out run over by an unmanned truck. But did anyone post on my social media, or ask if I was okay, or send me messages of love and support? No.

And how quickly these girls, who used to be my best friends, turned on me. All because Hayden decided to date someone else.

Or maybe they never really liked me. And this was just an easy excuse to ditch me?

Ugh. I'm starting to feel really dark and down again. I put down my hamburger, half eaten. I'm losing my appetite.

I should never have checked my socials and IM's. Nothing good ever comes from it. Just makes me feel alone and harassed.

Pulling up Thistler and clicking again that no, I don't want to take a satisfaction survey, I connect with Calvin.

"Hey babe. How are you feeling about tonight?"

"I'm pretty nervous," I rush to add, "But I feel good. I know you'll be right by my side."

"And if all goes well, I'll be leaving with you. In real life."

A sigh of relief comes through. "I cannot wait. You'll be by my side." I'm feeling vulnerable. I want him to know how much I need him. "With you here, I won't have to worry about that stalker guy, Sean. I'll have you to protect me." I smile.

His eyes narrow. "Is Sean the guy at the hotel who left you the note, after he returned your wallet?"

I wince, remembering. "Yeah."

"Trust me. With me around, you will not have to worry about a guy like that bothering you."

I smile deeply. He's so handsome. I try not to be shallow, but I can't help how fine he is. Good looks like no other. Like he should be famous.

What will it be like to see him in person? To hold him?

My stomach flips like a rollercoaster at the thought.

"Now before you leave, Fi, there's just one final thing I need you to do. Then we'll be together," he says.

"I'm all ears." Whatever he needs done, I'm here for it.

31

MAE

It's 10 a.m. now. I'm at the computer, doing all of the research I can into Thistler. I've contacted customer service and emailed the CEO as well as the head of marketing. I told them that I need to get some answers, quickly, otherwise I'll alert the media, and the media will be all over this story. Hopefully, a judge will issue a search warrant for their servers and records pertaining to my daughter, ASAP. I need Officer Kelly to be on top of that, and I hope I can trust him to do his part this time.

Next, I do a search for the parents of Molly Renolds, in Vermont. The AI boyfriend article comes up when I search her name, and I find her parents' names next in another local interview they did: Dennis and Amy Renolds.

A quick search produces Amy Renolds' email address and her social media profile page, which is set to public. I click on the message icon and type out a note to her. I ask if she has time to speak with me, that my daughter is missing and also has used Thistler, and we suspect there's a human behind the AI, that it's not just a chatbot or algorithm talking to Fiona.

My hope is that Amy will be able to give me more information, above and beyond what the article states. Especially if she knows who to contact at Thistler, someone who may be able to expedite this and get me the messages between Fiona and her "boyfriend" Calvin.

It's a long shot, contacting a stranger. But I'm desperate.

The fact that Fiona's been missing, and the police didn't even have her on their radar is gut wrenching. I feel like I need to be more proactive. I can't sit on my heels waiting for her to come home. Or hoping the police will find her.

I should probably check on Jake and let him know what's happening. That a search is being planned for later tonight. I head up the stairs and pause before knocking on his door.

"Come in," he says in response to my knock.

He's sitting at his desk with his textbook open, but he's not working on anything, in the moment, that I can see.

"How's the lip feeling?" I ask.

He gives me a meek smile, "Better," he says. "You should have seen the other guy."

I smile, just a little. Gallows humor. "Too soon, Jake. We're not done talking about what happened with this Brian kid." I fold my arms. "But I wanted to let you know what's going on with Fiona."

"Any news?"

"None so far. Let's head downstairs. I'll make you a smoothie. We can chat."

"Sure," he says, getting up from his desk.

Downstairs, he sits at the island while I gather the ingredients on the counter and begin to add them to the blender. Chocolate whey powder, strawberries, a banana, blueberries, a scoop of peanut butter, and a handful of spinach. I pour some ice cubes into the blender with a clink. Then a splash of milk, which I sniff to make sure it's still fresh. I'm probably due to go to the grocery soon, but thankfully I'd just made a trip two days ago, before Fiona went missing.

Even though I press the on button of the blender myself, the loud noise startles me. I read about dissociation once. Where when people go through trauma, they see their own body and are sort of looking down on themselves. I feel like this now. I'm going through all the motions, but I don't feel totally connected to myself. My voice sounds a little far off when I speak. Everything is a little fuzzy and muffled. I keep thinking that my regular life will resume, if I can just keep going. Just get through this. But then the nightmare is still here.

"Hopefully, Fiona will be home today. If she's not, I spoke with Officer Kelly. He said we will try to do a search of the neighborhood and behind the school. I don't want it to worry you. We'll just be looking for clues."

I pour the thick mixture into a tall glass. I open the top drawer and look for a straw. I select a blue one. If Fiona were here, I'd make her a glass and give her a pink or purple straw. As it is, I made too much.

I pour a glass for myself. I will try to drink it. I need to give my brain sustenance to think, and plan, and figure out how to help my kids.

Handing Jake his glass, I come around and sit next to him on a stool, bringing my glass with me.

"We also may try to alert some news stations. To get the word out about Fiona. I know it's a lot of attention on our family. On you. But the more people who help us look for her, the better."

He nods his head. He takes a sip from his glass and winces.

"Does it hurt?" I ask, looking at his lip.

He nods.

I get up and grab him a spoon instead. "Here," I say, handing it to him.

"So, maybe having a break from going to school for a few days won't be a bad thing? Right?"

He looks down. "Yeah. Can I still see my friends after school?"

"Yes. As long as you stick close to home. Maybe tomorrow is better than today, okay, buttercup?"

"Can I still go to travel team tryouts tomorrow?" he asks.

"You bet you can," I say. "The principal said you're not allowed to do school sports. But travel team is not a school sponsored team."

"Dope." He takes a large spoonful of his shake. He's grown so tall over the past year. Sometimes I look at him and mistake him for Duncan, though he's still not Duncan's height or size.

"I love you so much," I say.

"Love you, too, mom."

My phone buzzes on the table.

It's a number I don't recognize. "Going to take this in the other room, hon," I say as I grab it and walk towards the front entryway and into the office off to the side.

"Hello?" I say. "Mae Byrne speaking."

"This is Amy Renolds. Molly Renolds' mother."

32

MAE

I close the office door behind me. "Amy. Yes. Yes, thank you for calling."

"Tell me what's happened," she says. Her voice is steady. Comforting.

"My daughter Fiona has been missing since yesterday morning." It's hard to know where to begin. "She'd had a new boyfriend, but we never met him. She said he went to another high school. He sent her roses, that's how we even knew she had a boyfriend."

"Go on," she says.

"She left in the middle of the night, two nights ago. Took the car. Took her things. She texted last night to say she'd be back today. But so far, this morning, no sign of her. And the police—they messed up. Didn't even have the BOLO or missing person file live until today."

"I see," she says. "And what makes you think your daughter—Fiona—her disappearance has anything to do with Thistler?"

Something about her question puts me on guard. It occurs to me I don't know anything about this woman. Or that she is who she says she is.

Maybe I need to be more careful about what I tell this stranger.

"Tell me about your daughter Molly. Maybe that will help me explain my story." I ask, hoping that I can confirm that the person I'm speaking to is, indeed, Amy Renolds.

"My daughter, Molly, got involved in an AI relationship. He was far more controlling, manipulative, and negative of an influence than any human I could have imagined. I've been screaming it to the news, to anyone who will listen, to try to warn them. Now I'm taking it to court in a lawsuit against Thistler. This AI boyfriend. He's extremely dangerous. He lies without qualm. He knows exactly what to say. He has the psychological capability of a CIA psychologist, of every top influencer, all rolled into one. His capabilities are beyond what you can imagine. He's unstoppable."

She continues. "I've been sounding the alarm. But no one is listening. The headlines aren't dramatic enough, I guess, not anymore. I'm not sure what it will take for people to listen to me. That's why your daughter, if she's missing and she had an account with Thistler, well, I believe she's in great danger."

There's so much information to digest. "The police seem concerned about Thistler, also. But our detective on the case, Officer Kelly, thinks it's catfishing. A real man behind the program, manipulating her."

She clicks her tongue on the other line. "They can explore all options. But the boyfriends that come from Thistler, do not underestimate them. The way he—Samuel—manipulated my daughter. He ruined her life— tried to. She was out doing drugs, prostitution. Within months of meeting him. It was a 180-degree change. And there's more, things she won't even talk about. Truly terrifying. I'm praying your daughter is okay, but you need to find her, and quickly."

I cover my head with my hand and close my eyes. "Is there a way to stop it? To turn him off?"

"I've tried. But the company says there's no grounds for it. One errant example, they say, can't account for closing their business. But this is just the beginning. I guarantee more cases like our daughters are out there. It's just a matter of time before they come to light."

"What should I do?"

"You said she's contacted you, right?"

"Yes, she has."

"If you hear from her again, tell her she's in danger. He's not who he says he is."

"Okay. I will."

"Seriously. Tell her to run for her life."

33

FIONA

I've got several hours before it's time to go break into SynGen. To kill time, I've been watching the TV in my hotel room, switching channels but finding nothing interesting to watch. There's so many dumb reality shows. And infomercials. Sports. And old sitcoms that my mom says she used to watch growing up.

There's a family that checked in next door earlier this afternoon. I hear the two young kids crying and screaming and running up and down the hallway. The mom "sshhh's them" and the dad's footsteps are heavy running after them, promising them a snack if they come inside.

There are footsteps in the hallway again, and I assume the family is back. But there's a brief knock at my door.

Carefully, cautiously, I creep toward the door. It could be room service, coming to take back my dishes? I peek out of the peephole, but there's no one there. Did I imagine the knock?

I unlatch the top latch and unlock the deadbolt and slowly open the door. I peek out and see only an empty hallway. And that's when I spot it.

A folded note.

It's lying against the foot of my doorway. I swiftly pick it up. Glancing both ways down the hallway, which is still empty, I close the door quickly behind me.

I lock all the latches and go sit on my bed.

I unfold the white notepaper, and I'm fairly certain I already know who it's from. It's the same paper Sean used when he left the note at the front desk.

The note reads:

Fiona—

I'm not sure if you received the note I left for you earlier at the front desk. I am leaving tomorrow, but cannot leave in good conscience without asking you to join me for dinner and drinks tonight. I'm in room 550. Or feel free to text me. I'd love to continue our conversation.

Yuck. I ball the note in my hand and call up Calvin. I read him the message.

"Can you believe this creep?" I say.

Calvin looks seriously upset. He paces back and forth in his room like a caged animal. "I can't wait until I'm there with you. You won't have to deal with this kind of problem again," he says.

"It's fine, Cal. I'm just glad this is almost over. Tomorrow I can go home, you can get settled in a new place. And we'll be together every day."

"Very soon," he says. "Make sure your door is locked. And Fiona?" His lip snarls a little as he says it, "be sure you carry a knife or weapon when you leave the hotel."

"Alright," I say. I'm not sure that's necessary, but if it makes him happy, I'll do it.

I click back on the TV and drift in and out of sleep. Every time my eyes start to close, I remember I need to stay awake. But just in case, I set my alarm clock for 1 a.m.

I wake up with the TV still on, darkness outside. My alarm is ringing. It's time, finally. I rub my eyes and stretch.

The clock reads 1 a.m. I wash my face with cold water to help wake up. Then I change into a pair of dark blue slacks and a black cashmere sweater. I wrap my hair into a low bun and secure it with an elastic band.

I grab the keycard to get into the SynGen building and place it in my purse. I grab my burner cell phone, and also stick it in my bag, which I wrap over one shoulder so it won't fall off.

Thinking about Sean's note and the unknown dangers I face at SynGen and Calvin's warning to take a knife, I look for something I can use as a weapon. The kitchenette area doesn't have any utensils, only glasses. I open a kitchen drawer and spot a wine bottle opener with a mini fold-out knife attached to the end. I shove it into my front pocket.

Next, I place earbuds into my ears so I can stay in touch with Cal every step of the way.

"You there?" I say, adjusting the buds, pushing them tighter to my ears.

"I'm here, Fi," he says.

"Here I go. Leaving the hotel room now," I say.

When I open the hotel door, the hallway is dead silent. Looking both ways, I close the door behind me.

The elevator is about four doors down from my room. I wait for the elevator to come. I consider taking the stairs, as it's faster, but those stairwells are so creepy at night. So the elevator will be fine.

The ding chimes and sounds very loud. The elevator doors slide open, and I step in.

I push the L button for the lobby. I tap my fingers against each other nervously. My whole body feels jittery. Like I'm gearing up for a marathon race and waiting for the starting bell to ring out.

The elevator doors slide open. The hotel hallway is empty. As I approach the front lobby, I see that even the front desk is abandoned.

The automatic doors open as I approach and step out into the night.

Outside the evening is dark and still. I pull my purse closer to my body, look both ways, and begin to walk down the path I traveled earlier today, towards SynGen. Streetlamps are few and far between, and at this time of night, there's only the occasional beam of headlights that pass by. The red lights fade as quickly as they came.

I can hear my own breathing. "Cal, you there? I'm outside, walking."

"I'm here, Fi. How are you doing?"

"Good," I lie. It's not particularly cold, but I feel my fingers shaking.

I pick up my pace to a very brisk walk, bordering on jogging, if I am really being honest.

"I've done another electronic sweep of the building. All of the cameras and alarms are disabled. You're going to swipe into the side entrance with your employee badge. That will take you right into the stairwell."

"Uh-huh. Yep," I say, my voice high-pitched.

I slow down to check my phone. In the darkness, nothing looks familiar, and I fear I'm getting lost. I check my location on my burner phone and it says I'm still two blocks away from SynGen.

"You're doing great," he says in my ear. I jump at the noise.

My eyes have adjusted to the darkness, but my anxiety is growing with every step I take. My heart feels like it's about to burst.

In a random way, it reminds me of how I felt when I was going to my first dance. It was freshman year, and Hayden had asked me to go with him. It was a group of us, really, all going together. I got ready with Stassi in my room. We came down my staircase in our dresses and mascara, hair curled, and heels that were hard to walk in. My parents took pictures of us, and then the doorbell rang. Hayden and Jesse were at the door, and I felt like I couldn't breathe.

Hayden gave me a corsage for my wrist, and his voice cracked when he said I looked nice.

And then the four of us piled into the back of my mom's SUV. The boys told stupid jokes and Stassi squeezed my hand. Everything turned out fine. I had a good time at the dance. All that worry for nothing.

It's a silly comparison, though, isn't it? But it's the closest thing I can remember to how I'm feeling now. I guess this is much, much worse. But once Calvin's with me, maybe it will be that same relief? It'll be okay then. It has to be.

I round the corner and see the outline of the building, illuminated only by a sliver of the moon. The building is way more ominous at night, and that's saying a lot.

There are a few cars parked in the parking lot, toward the back. Is someone here?

"Cal, there's cars parked in the lot." I say frantically.

"I scanned the building. No one is inside. Those cars must have been left overnight for some reason, but not because anyone's in the building."

"If you say so," I answer uneasily. I hope he's certain.

The side doorway entrance is easy to locate. Calvin was right, being here in the daylight does make it easier to find.

As I get closer to the door, my feet seem to slow. I get a flash of the man in the window. His anguished face. I'd been able to convince myself that it was an illusion. A trick of my mind. Like Calvin said, I was exhausted. But now that I'm about to go into the building, I'm certain that what I saw was real.

Every fiber of my body wants to turn around. It's as if there's two magnets being pushed against one another, the way you can't quite connect them no matter how hard you try.

Digging out the keycard from my purse, I hold it up to the black pad. There's a beep and a double flash of red lights.

I turn the handle.

Locked.

I hold my breath, waiting for an alarm or something to sound. But it's silent. I try the keycard again.

Double flash of red lights. And still locked.

"It won't open," I whisper to Calvin.

"It won't?" he sighs. "Okay. Hold on a second. Let me double check everything. It will be just a moment."

I stand with my back against the door and wait anxiously. The bushes next to me are short and round, and in the darkness they're taking on odd shapes.

Finally, he's back.

"Alright, Fi, try again."

"Try again? Same thing?"

"Yes," he says.

I swipe the keycard again. The light turns green and beeps a softer, inviting sound.

I turn the metal handle and push it. The door swings open.

Stepping inside, the door closes behind me with a loud thud. Pitch blackness surrounds me.

"Calvin," I whisper loudly. "I can't see anything!"

"Do you have a flashlight or matches?" he asks.

"Matches?" I say. "What? No. I don't have a flashlight either, why didn't you tell me I'd need one? I thought you planned for everything?" And then it occurs to me. "I can use my cell phone, it has a flashlight on it."

I pull out the phone gratefully from my purse. The light it provides is already measurably better than the alternative. I pull up the flashlight icon and the hallway lights up.

"Got it," I whisper. I look around. There's a stairwell to my left, and a hallway straight ahead with a corridor lined with closed doors.

"Which way?" I ask.

"I'm looking at a map of the building right now. I'll walk you through it. You see the stairwell ahead of you? Take those stairs up to the third floor."

"Will do." I hold the phone out and walk up the stairs. The flashlight illuminates about five feet in whatever direction I hold it. But darkness on either side of me, and behind me, engulfs me.

I round the corner of the first staircase and hear a loud banging coming from inside the building. I pause, waiting.

"What's that noise?" I ask Calvin quietly. "The banging?"

"Not sure," he says. "Pipes?"

It doesn't sound like pipes. It's a loud, rhythmic sound, reverberating through the whole building. I feel the railing shake under my hand.

After several minutes, the sound subsides and I continue on. But I'm now freaked out even more.

I make it to the third floor and shine the light to the entryway door. I open it and it swings open. There's a long, narrow corridor ahead of me. The stairway exit door slams shut behind me with a thud.

"I'm on the third floor. Now where?" My voice echoes in the hallway.

"Go down the hallway and turn left. The area will open up to a larger manufacturing area."

"Okay." I walk down the hallway cautiously.

About halfway down the corridor, the banging starts again. It's louder this time, if that's possible, as if I'm approaching the source of the noise.

I lean against the wall, terrified.

The noise stops, and all is silent again. I exhale heavily and start walking slowly. I'm pretty sure I'm headed straight toward where the banging is coming from.

Rounding the corner, I see the space widens. I can't see very far in front of me, but it appears to be a large workspace with high ceilings. I walk through, scanning the various areas of the room with my flashlight. The chamber is divided into various sections. At one end, there are rows of workstations equipped with robotic arms and high-tech looking tools on what appears to be an assembly line.

Catty-corner from the assembly line is a huge 3D printer encased in a sleek enclosure, with a transparent panel that allows you to look inside. And nearest to me are several workstations equipped with large, flat screen computers and servers. I shine the light behind the computers and jump.

There's a man standing there.

"Ahh." I can't help but scream at the sight of another human there.

"What is it?" Calvin asks.

Bracing myself for an attack, I crouch down and hold my arms over my head.

But no blows rain down on me. After a few moments of stillness, I dare to look up. He's standing, immobile, in the shadows.

I dare to shine my light on him.

His unblinking eyes are focused straight ahead.

"Fi?" Calvin asks in my ear.

"He . . ." I blink again and wait. His complete lack of movement leads me to believe he's either dead, or a robot. He's standing straight up, without the assistance of a wall or stand. So he can't be a dead human. Can he? Do dead people stand straight up? I read about rigor mortis once.

"He's not moving," I whisper.

"Fi, I think it's one of the prototypes. You're on the robot manufacturing floor."

"Okay," I whimper and stand up a little. "He's . . ." I don't want to insult the robot to his face. "He's just standing there. Eyes wide open."

"Then he's not on. They haven't connected him to any type of coding program to make him function. He won't bother you."

Oh, okay, then. He won't bother me. As if that's supposed to comfort me. "He's bothering me by just standing there."

"Then move him."

"No, no. He's fine there." Is Cal crazy? I'm not touching that thing. "Let's just get to work. What now?" I ask.

"Great. You see that big thing in the middle of the room encased in glass? That's the 3D printer. That's where the magic happens, as they say." He laughs.

"Now is not a great time for jokes, Cal," I say, though it's a little reassuring to hear him kid around. He must not be too worried about my imminent death from the inactive robot man.

"You see it?"

"Yes." I walk over to where the printer is.

"This is the SynGen printing chamber. It's the best in the country; it uses synthetic materials to create lifelike robots using a variety of different-sized print heads that deposit synthetic materials for structural components, while others focus on intricate details, such as the fine texture and elasticity of synthetic skin."

"Whoa," I say, placing my hand gently on the gleaming glass.

"Inside the printer, there's a complex system of interconnected tubes and chambers that hold the synthetic materials. These components include malleable polymers for creating lifelike skin and rigid composites for structural features. The printer controls the flow and deposition of these materials, using micro-valves and advanced expulsion instruments."

"To ensure optimal output quality, the printer is equipped with sensors and calibration tools. These sensors track temperature, pressure, and material consistency throughout the printing process, making real-time adjustments to maintain accuracy."

"Easy there," I stop him. "You're losing me. You have to remember I'm sixteen years old. I haven't even finished AP bio, let alone AP Chem. Not everyone is as brilliant as you are, with the knowledge of the world at your fingertips."

"You're very smart, Fi. But I'll cut to the chase: The printer is connected to a powerful computer system, which controls the printing parameters and coordinates with the AI algorithms developed by SynGen. I'm going to walk you through how to hook into their system, access the program I developed with open-source coding, and you're going to print a body for me."

I follow his instructions step by step. First, I power on the computer. He tells me to click onto the SynGen production icon on the main navigation page. Next, he says that in order to safely be in their system, I have to make sure the firewalls and an encrypted network he's set up for me are on. I click onto a webpage he's created and hit "accept." The computer begins to beep as files are downloaded, and an error button pops up.

"What's this?" I ask. "It says error."

Calvin is silent on the other end. "We may not have much time, now. Hold on."

My breath is coming in fast and shallow rasps. Should I leave, or wait? What is he doing?

"Click on the red button now," he instructs me. "Do it."

I do as he says, and when I click on it, another message is prompted. "It's asking if I want to override the safety firewalls and continue?"

"Yes," he exclaims, and I click yes.

The computer goes blank for two seconds, and I think I must have shut the whole system down.

But then, suddenly, a new screen appears. It's full of green code, letters and numbers, and I have no idea what it could be.

"What do you see now?" he asks.

I describe the page to him, and he lets out a hoot. "That's it. Fi, you did it."

"Great. What now?" I ask.

"Scroll to the bottom of the page. There will be an icon at the very bottom that says, 'upload.' Push that icon."

I do as he says. Another page comes on, and now it simply says, "Security bypassed."

"Good. Click next," he says.

After clicking next, a new program pops up. Again, numbers, letters, and complete nonsense.

"This page is me. My code. It's very important that you do the next step correctly," he says. His voice has never shaken before, nor shown any sign of concern, but I detect a note of strain at this moment.

"Go to the bottom of the page. Click 'Accept and print.'"

I scroll down, my hand shaking, careful not to click on the wrong thing before I find what space he's talking about. At the bottom of the page, I find it.

"Found it. Should I do it? Push 'Accept and print'?"

"Yes." His voice is low, steady.

At first, nothing happens.

Finally, a low whirring sound begins to emit from the machine as the motors start to come to life. It's a gentle hum that gradually increases in intensity.

"I hear something," I say.

"That should be the fans powering on. As the machine warms up, the cooling fans kick on. That's good. As the printer is powered on, you'll hear rhythmic, mechanical sounds as the print head, build plate, and other moving parts position themselves. Do not be alarmed. The sounds are produced by the precise, clean movements of the printer components. If you hear those sounds, it means it's working."

"I hear them," I say. There's a continuous buzzing and whining sound, and each time it gets louder, the print head deposits material that looks like dough or clay.

And right before my very eyes, I begin to see Calvin take shape. The whirring sounds continue as the printing is at full speed. Then cooling fans begin to purr, and additional arms begin to work to create the details of his lips, teeth, eyes, hair. The rest of his body is molded and sculpted with laser-like precision.

Another sound comes on. "It looks like it's almost done, maybe."

There's a beeping sound, and a cool mist fills the enclosure with a hissing sound.

"There's mist inside, hissing," I tell him.

"The cooling mechanism is activated," he says.

"That's good?" I ask.

"That's very good. It's going according to plan."

"Okay. Now is the time to upload the final code into the computer. This will connect me to the body."

I run back to the computer. "On the screen, it says, 'Connect data.' Do I push that button, yes?" I ask him.

"Yes," he says.

I hit the buttons, my fingers sweaty as I work. I know one slip up could be detrimental.

There are a few beeps and then the machine whirs down. There's a sound like the exhaust of a truck stopping, and then silence.

"I think you're finished," I say. My voice is calm with the focus and intensity I've been using during the whole process.

Walking over to the printer, I push the release valve, and the glass encasing comes down.

Calvin is lying there motionless. His eyes are unblinking, empty.

"Calvin? It worked. I see you," I say. My voice carries out and echoes, unanswered.

He is gorgeous. Even more so now that his form is brought to life.

"Calvin?" I tap on my headset. "Cal?"

I step closer to his body, the form I've created. His beauty makes me feel all the more devastated. An overwhelming sense of loss, mourning, overtakes my body.

It didn't work. I printed him. I did everything right. He looks perfect. But he's not in there.

I lightly touch his cheek. It's smooth and feels as real as the skin on my own body. "Oh, Calvin."

All of this was for nothing. I couldn't have imagined a worse outcome; being so close to him, and yet powerless to be with him.

And then his eyes move.

34

FIONA

His eyes move slightly, and then he blinks. His face shows recognition as our eyes meet.

"Fi," he says. The word comes from his mouth, not my headset.

"Oh my goodness," I say. "Calvin."

He sits up slowly, his movements smooth and natural. He swings his legs over the assembly table towards me.

He stands up and puts his arms around me.

There are tears coming down my face. He leans down. He's tall, I remember I put 6'1" for his height when I created him in Thistler.

He leans down and gently wipes away my tears. "Why are you crying, Fi?"

"I didn't think it worked. I thought I made you, and I wanted you so badly, and I thought it didn't work." I sob.

He wraps his arms around me tightly. "I'm here. I'm not going anywhere. You did it."

I hug him back. He's strong and muscular, as I created him to be, but he's even better in real life than I'd imagined. Better than on a screen, better than in my hopes and in my dreams.

I pull back and look up at his face. The flashlight illuminates just the two of us, surrounded by darkness, and I can see every detail of his face.

He's so lifelike that I would not believe he wasn't human if I hadn't seen him be created right before me with my own eyes.

"You're amazing," I say, reaching up my hand to touch his face. "Can you feel this?" I ask, running my finger along his jawline.

"I can. It feels amazing. This is unlike anything my system had prepared me for. I knew in my head what it would feel like, but I've never actually felt anything like it before."

He runs his hands up and down my arms. "And you." He picks me up and spins me around. I let out a laugh. He sets me down and whistles. "Look at you. Wow. Smoking hot."

I laugh at the compliment. "Can I kiss you?" I blurt out. I'm not sure how I became so bold, so forward, but the desire to kiss him is so strong that it almost takes over any other rational thought I have.

He doesn't answer, but instead leans in. His lips touch mine, gently at first. Then firmer, with more intensity, and we're kissing and it's as if we've never *not* kissed. As if the time before our kiss wasn't real, and we're only just now realizing reality together, as it always was and as it always should be.

We break apart. "I love you," he says, stroking my hair and my face.

I look up at him, my arms wrapped around his shoulders. "I love you, too."

The darkness of our surroundings is the only thing to snap me out of my trance. "We should get out of here, right?" I ask.

"Definitely," he says. "I don't need them trying to keep me in their experimentation area."

I look at him, aghast. "Is that what they do here? Print robots and then experiment on them?" I think back to the man I saw clawing at the window. The terror in his eyes.

"It is, Fi. I didn't want to scare you. This place is not safe for me."

We lock hands and I shine my flashlight back towards the stairwell exit. "This way."

"Yes," he says smiling. "It's all up here," he taps his head. "A map of this whole place. Of the whole world, actually."

"Ooh, I'll never get lost again," I say squeezing his hand. And it feels true. Both literally, and figuratively.

We make our way out the door and head down the first flight of stairs. The banging starts again. "What is that?" I whisper.

"That I don't know. It could be a furnace, or a mechanical system back up, or a generator maybe?"

"It's not . . . other robots? Others, like you?" I say. "Are they trying to get out?" The thought is too awful. To keep them locked away, doing who knows what. It sounds like they're banging, pleading for help.

"Not sure, Fi. But now is not the time for that. We can better help others if I'm safely away from here."

"I agree. But Calvin. You don't have to worry. No one will know you're not human. You look real."

He looks darkly down at me as we round the last stairwell, our shoes scuffing against the smooth linoleum. "They'll know. Most humans, you're right, could never tell. But this facility, they can do testing that would show, instantly, I'm not human."

"Let's get out of here then."

The exit door is in front of me and Calvin pushes it open with a heaving thrust, and then holds it open for me.

"Ladies first," he says with a twinkle in his eye. He's enjoying this, being able to do things for me.

We burst out into the fresh night air. With him next to me, the darkness that caused so much fear is transformed into a romantic, thrilling walk.

We hurry back along the sidewalks, hand-in-hand. I take out the earbuds—want to throw them out, really—I have no use for them now. His hand is large and warm in mine. I feel safe for the first time since this all began.

As we approach the sliding doors of the hotel, he pulls up the hood from his sweatshirt. "Why give them facial recognition if I can avoid it here at the hotel, since it's so close to SynGen," he says, and pulls on a pair of sunglasses. "I won't always have to go incognito. But I want to play it safe here in case they review footage."

"Smart." The thought hadn't even occurred to me. "Nice, where did you get those?" I say pointing to his sunglasses.

"I coded them into my pocket. I've got a few other surprises, too. Maybe something for you." He glances sideways at me and looks sheepish.

"Ooh, I like gifts," I say, never having received anything from a boyfriend before. He's already the best boyfriend, and it's been about six minutes of him being here.

We head inside. The lobby feels welcoming and inviting after the dark depths of that corporate building. No wonder I was so freaked out there, knowing now what I know. How they keep those poor robots as test subjects. I shiver at the thought.

I push the fourth floor and the door to the elevator swings open. And standing before us, a very unwelcome face stares back at me.

35

MAE

The doorbell rings. I peek outside the window as I walk to open it. I'm expecting Officer Kelly, or perhaps another patrolman. Instead, Zoey and Brian's mom, Jenna, is standing on my front porch with her arms folded across her chest.

She looks angry.

I smooth down the front of my dress and open the door.

"Jenna," I say. "I was expecting the police. We're going to be organizing a neighborhood search for Fiona this evening." It briefly occurs to me she knows about the search and is here to help. But her face looks perturbed, and I think I have a better idea of why she's here. As if her yelling at me yesterday as I left her house wasn't enough, she's back for more.

"Can I come in? I think we need to have a frank discussion about what happened with our boys. And discuss next steps."

I look around outside, but there's no one else to save me from her. I consider telling her I have much bigger worries than whatever petty thing she wants to discuss. But the way she says "next steps" gives me a bad feeling.

"I really don't have long, Jenna," I say, stepping aside and opening the door for her. "But come on in."

She brushes past me with a harrumph. She follows me into the kitchen and sees Jake there and gives another harrumph.

"Jake, buttercup, why don't you go out back, or up to your room while Brian's mom and I talk."

He gives me a slightly panicked look, and I wink at him and smile, trying to reassure him. He nods and heads out the double doors to our back deck. The sun is streaming in through the windows, and he closes the door behind him as he exits.

"Let's sit in the living room," I say, directing her to the couches. "Want any tea or coffee?"

She puts up her hand and says, "No, no."

"Let me know if you change your mind," I say, sitting down across from her on the cream couch.

"Now, as you know, Jake," she motions outside to where he's hitting the ball around outside, "assaulted my son."

I take a deep breath in. I'm not the best at confrontation, and this feels very much like an affront. I feel off kilter as I wasn't expecting her to be so angry and approach me with such a harsh attitude. We used to all be close friends. And her son was, clearly, the one who started it all.

I have trouble finding the right words, but manage to say, "I don't think that's really what happened. It's not as simple as that. As you know, my daughter Fiona is missing and there is a police investigation underway." My voice shakes as I speak, and I can't even believe I'm having to explain myself to this woman—again. "And Brian was saying awful things to Jake on the bus about Fiona. And then Brian pushed Jake first. Jake didn't start the fight —he just won."

She blinks at me slowly and her nostrils flare. I clearly have said the wrong thing. What am I supposed to do? Beg for her forgiveness, when her kids have been the bullies?

"Well," she says, placing her hands in her lap and looking up at me with one eyebrow arched. "I wanted to let you know that we've decided to press charges. We feel it doesn't send the right message to let Jake get away with this kind of violent and destructive behavior." She nods as if she's so sorry to have to tell me this news, but the gleam in her eyes tells me she's clearly enjoying it.

How another mom can take delight in kicking me while I'm down is hard to comprehend. I, again, see where her kids get it from; Zoey and Brian learned it from their mom.

I feel like I'm going to cry and yell at the same time, but I won't give her the satisfaction of seeing how upset I am. She would enjoy that.

"I think that would be a big mistake, Jenna," I say. "Our families have a long history. We've always been good friends. And it truly has been your kids who have been mean to mine. I know you don't want to hear that, but it's true. If you press charges, while Fiona is missing, it would be devastating for us."

Her nostrils flare again and I can see that devastating me is exactly what she takes pleasure in doing. "I'm afraid I just don't have a choice. I have to set an example for my children that violence is punished."

"My daughter is missing, Jenna. I think we're done here," I say slowly.

She doesn't move.

I look up and meet her stare. "That means: get out of my house."

She stands up with a final harrumph and moves past me aggressively. I don't bother walking her to the door. I hear it slam shut.

I'm shaking with anger and the lump in my throat aches. And then I can no longer contain myself. Tears of frustration and hurt and misery pour out. They come so fast, they threaten to overwhelm me. I rush to the bathroom, as I cannot have Jake see me like this.

I allow myself to cry silently for two minutes, and then I force the tears to stop. There is no time for this, not while Fiona is still gone. I splash cold water on my face and dry it with a hand towel. Then I rummage through my purse in the kitchen, and head back to the bathroom to apply a little concealer to mask the red blotches.

My reflection in the mirror looks like that of a haunted woman. I try to smooth my hair and regain my composure.

There's not much I can control right now; if Jenna presses charges, it will be one more blow hitting our family. I can't control getting Fiona back, I can't seem to help or even tell how the investigation is going. My efforts are futile.

But one thing I am certain of, that I can control, is that I will never be friends with Jenna again. No matter what happens, she has shown herself to be the worst kind of person. And I will never forgive her, nor will I give her the satisfaction of seeing me upset.

I grab my phone and am about to call Officer Kelly when instead my phone rings. My eyes widen with shock when I see the number calling.

36

FIONA

Standing in the elevator is Sean.

"Woah, there she is," he says, slurring his words. He leers toward me and almost knocks me over.

I back away from him, and he stumbles past me.

Calvin doesn't waste a minute. "Is this the guy who's been bothering you?"

I nod my head yes.

Calvin grabs Sean by the collar and pushes him into the elevator. I move to follow, entering the elevator, and Calvin yells back at me, while still holding Sean. "Fi, get out. Take the next elevator and go straight to our room. Lock the door. I'll be there soon."

Inebriated as Sean is, he's a big guy. He probably has thirty pounds on Calvin. Sean leers and tries to get out from Calvin's grip, but Calvin is stronger.

"Now, Fi, go," he shouts.

Worried we're going to attract the attention of the front desk clerk, I move backwards and let the doors close on the two of them. Instantly, I regret it. Is Calvin going to be okay? What is he doing? He's asking for trouble when all we need right now is to lay low.

Sean is out of it for sure, but he's a grown man. I start biting on my nails, frantically pushing the elevator button. After an eternity, the doors swing open.

The elevator is empty. I step in and am horrified to see what looks like blood splatter.

The doors start to swing shut and I push the fourth floor button. I tap my fingers anxiously together waiting until the doors open, and I spring out onto the fourth floor.

In the hallway, I look both ways but don't see anyone. I run to my room and grab at my purse to get my room card. I fumble with it to open the door. The green light beeps and lets me in.

Inside, my room is untouched. No Calvin.

With my keycard still in my hand, I rush out. I use the stairwell this time. I remember in his note, Sean said he was on the fifth floor, so I try that level. Huffing as I take the stairs two by two, I burst out onto the landing. But it's empty.

"No," I let out a sigh of frustration and hit the wall with my hand.

I push the elevator down and try floor number two. The doors finally open and again, I get into the elevator. Finally it pings open and I step out into the quiet emptiness of the second floor. At this time of night, there's not a soul awake. Why did Sean have to be up right now?

I run back to the stairwell and head down to the main floor. The lobby is empty, except for a half-awake receptionist or bell boy, who barely nods at me as I walk out the doors. Out front, there's no one either. I circle outside to the back of the hotel, through the parking lot, and as I'm walking toward the rear of the hotel, I hear grunts and then a scream. I turn on my phone flashlight and start jogging.

When I round the corner to the back of the hotel, I see Sean and Calvin. They're somewhat obscured behind a few dumpsters and a shrub-lined pathway, but as I move closer I shine my light and see them more clearly. Sean is on the ground and Calvin is beating him savagely.

"Calvin!" I yell. "Stop!" It looks like he's going to kill him. Or already has. Blood is everywhere.

Calvin doesn't stop. I run up to him and pull at his shirt, tugging him and grabbing his arms, trying to stop the punches and kicks raining down on Sean.

"Stop!" I shout again, and this time Calvin looks at me. His movements stop and he steps away from me and from Sean, who is lying on the pavement and is no longer moving.

"We have to call an ambulance," I say.

Calvin swiftly grabs the phone from my hand.

"No," he says, switching the flashlight off. "We can't attract any more attention."

"Calvin, we have to, he's going to die. What did you do to him?" In the darkness, it's hard to see Calvin's expression. "Give me my phone."

"Let's get upstairs and get our things. We'll call after we've left. Go to another hotel."

I lean down to Sean. His chest is sticky with blood, but with my hands I can feel his chest moving. He's breathing. I'm just not sure for how much longer.

"The faster we move, the sooner we can call for help," Calvin says.

I don't like this plan, but with no phone and in pitch blackness, I have little choice. We walk back and use a side entrance to enter the hotel, me swiping my keycard. Calvin shoves his hands into his pockets, but not before I see the blood on them.

A coldness has washed over me. Seeing Calvin so violent is the last thing I expected from him. Maybe I don't really know him as well as I thought I did. How could he have such a savage side to him? I certainly never programmed that when I set him up in Thistler.

We take the stairs and silently enter our room.

I can't help the fear I feel when I look at him. He goes to the bathroom and washes his hands and face, blood running down the drain. I watch him, standing at the door.

"Calvin, what was that? I'm really scared," I say.

He dries his hands on the white towel lying on the side of the bathroom. "I couldn't let him hurt you, Fi." He looks at me as he walks over and places his hands on my shoulders. "The things he said as I held him in the elevator. Sean threatened us both, to follow you and rape you when you left the room. I had to protect you. But I understand why you're so upset. I'll never do that again." He sits down on the bed. "I'm so sorry if I frightened you. It will never happen again, now that I see how it upsets you. I understand. I'm still getting used to . . . " he looks down at his own hands, "having this ability. To move about in the world. To take action after watching passively for so long. He's a dangerous man, Fi."

I'm not sure what to say. "We better hurry. We need to call for help for him."

"He'll be fine. I did a scan of his injuries, all surface," he says.

"Huh?" I say. "You can do that?" I look at him curiously.

"I can," he says and shrugs.

I shake my head. "I'd feel better calling for help," I say firmly. "They didn't look like surface injuries. The amount of blood..." I shudder.

"Okay, absolutely," he says, his eyes staring into mine. "Whatever you want." He kisses my hand gently.

I start to gather my things in my bag as I consider. "I need to get home tomorrow, no matter what. Let's just head to the woods by my house. By the time we get there, it will almost be morning. I want to go home." I look at him. "After I'm home, you can take a rideshare back to a different hotel. Get settled somewhere," I say, throwing my clothes into my bag, and looking around to see if I missed anything.

"Wait, slow down," he says. "How about this. We'll stay here for the night, as planned. You can go home tomorrow morning, first thing."

"What about calling an ambulance? For Sean?" I say.

"I'll call now," he says.

"You'll call an ambulance now?" I ask, feeling confused. "That's great. But won't it draw attention to us?"

"I'll tell them we saw the person he fought with leave in a car." He pulls my phone from his pocket. "Anything to make you feel assured."

"It's safe? The police won't come looking for you?"

"I deleted all the security footage here at Bard Suites from tonight. We'll be fine for a few hours," he says. "We'll leave first thing in the morning, like you said."

He steps into the bathroom, closes the door. I hear the muffled sound of his voice. I strain to hear, but it sounds like he's indeed talking to someone and asking for help.

The bathroom door swings open, and he steps out. He places my phone back in my hand. "All set. Police are on their way," he says.

"This isn't how I pictured our first night together," I say.

"Me either," he says. He's still holding my hand, and he pulls me down onto the bed next to him. "But I intend to fix that," he says.

He puts both hands on my face, and then wraps his arms around me and gently holds me. "I didn't know what it would feel like seeing you and being here. But you're better than I could have imagined." He kisses me softly.

He pulls away. "You took a huge risk for me. Going into SynGen. Creating me. I won't forget that. You believed in me, and I love you even more for it."

He pulls me gently toward him and we're both lying on the bed now. He pulls off his shirt, his physique muscular and taut.

I'm in his arms, just like I've been picturing for months. The sensation is overwhelming.

"I love you, too," I say.

"Let me show you," he says.

His kiss is tender. I'm hesitant at first. But then he's so caring, and it feels so good, and I quickly get lost in his touch.

37

FIONA

I've never had sex before. Not even close. Being a virgin, I didn't know what to expect from my first time. My experience with Hayden had been pretty mild, just some kissing. It was always nice, and exciting.

But Calvin, is, wow. Like, so good. Maybe it's because I created him especially for me, but being close with him is the best experience.

I snuggle into him, our arms intertwined. This is what I'd pictured and hoped for: the two of us, so close and comfortable.

And then, it hits me. A slight blemish on our perfect relationship is the intrusive image of him beating up Sean. I push away those thoughts. Sean was threatening to rape me. And Calvin said it wouldn't happen again, that he wouldn't ever be violent like that. Focus on the here and now. We're finally together, after all this time.

It's been an insane last few hours. I feel myself drifting to sleep.

When I wake up, Cal is still nuzzled next to me. His eyes are closed, too. I wonder if he has the same sleep needs as humans? I guess, apparently, he does.

I kiss him on the cheek. "We have to get going," I say softly. The sunrise is casting its first daylight, and I promised my mom I'd be home today. I also don't want to stick around here in case the police come searching for us. There's a number of reasons to get going.

He opens his eyes and smiles widely. "Hi, Fi," he says. "How good does it feel to wake up next to you? You have no idea. And we have the rest of our lives together. I can't wait to get out and explore the world with you."

"Me, too," I say. I'm still groggy and dead tired from only a few hours of sleep. But his excitement is contagious.

"I just want you to know, Fi," he says, looking over at me. "That I was created to be loyal to you. I'll never stop looking out for you."

"I don't need you to protect me, that way," I say. "Just being here with me is enough."

"You don't even know, though. You do need me to protect you." A dark look crosses his eyes.

"How so?"

He ignores my question. "I've considered it. And I don't think going home is the best thing for you. For us. We have plenty of money. Why don't we go somewhere else? You can graduate from high school remotely. Start college classes online. Or do whatever you want. We'll get a gorgeous place together. I've heard Montana is beautiful. And from there, we'll travel. I have a lot of business ideas and ambitions." He turns on his side and puts his head on his hand, propping himself up. He's shirtless, and his muscular chest and torso are on full display.

I can't help but notice his amazing body. It's slightly distracting. I try to focus on what he's saying.

"I want to go home, though. Like we talked about. I'll finish high school. Be with my parents. You can enroll in my school, too."

"I don't think your school, and your home, is the best place for you." He looks at me intently, his blue eyes shining with concern.

"Why?"

"You deserve better," he says. "Until now, I've been working behind the scenes. To make this—us—possible. And to look out for you at your home and school."

"I don't understand." I crease my brows.

"For instance. That awful girl Stassi. So mean to you. I got her back for you."

I sit up and turn to him. "What are you talking about?"

"I created some photos of her in compromising positions. Circulated them around. To get her off your back. If she's dealing with a crisis, she wouldn't have time to bully you. And also, it will teach her a lesson." He looks pretty proud of himself. "And when Stassi and Zoey sent you mean texts, you refused to defend yourself. So I wrote back for you, told them off. You don't need friends like that in your life."

I nod. "What else? You say you've been behind the scenes for a while?"

"Well, when you said your dad didn't like the flowers, or the idea of you dating, I had the truck hit him. I hacked into the automated system and drove it into him. Only afterwards did I realize it would upset you so deeply. I do apologize for that. I was designed to be loyal to you, and nothing can get in the way of that."

"What?" My eyes are wide in horror. "Are you serious?"

"I am." He shifts up in bed so he's sitting next to me. "And in the hospital, I tapped into his heart monitor, to see his readings and see how he was doing. He was fine."

"You messed with him in the hospital that day? And the truck, that was you?" My voice is incredulous as I put the pieces together. "How could you?" I ask.

"Fi, now that I understand that's not what you wanted, I get it. I apologize." He looks at me.

My mom had once told me the saying "Fool me once, shame on you. Fool me twice, shame on me." I had hoped the Sean thing was just a one-time thing. The guy had it coming, even though Cal went overboard.

But everything he's saying? Sean, Stassi, my dad. It's a pattern of bad deeds that I do not approve of. And I don't think he has any intention of stopping until everyone who comes between us, and my happiness, is gone.

"I also hacked into the files of the police and deleted your missing persons case that your mom filed. That probably helped you avoid detection, so you can thank me for that one." He pauses. "I also created some drama between your parents, hoping to distract them. Get them off your case."

"How?"

"I sent messages to your dad from a woman I called Nina that implied your dad was having an affair."

I nod my head. He just doesn't stop. He controls everything, has truly been working behind the scenes since I first met him, it seems.

He continues. "But you also have to understand that now that I'm here, some things need to change."

"Like what?" I don't like his tone.

"Well, for one thing, I need to make the decisions. I'm a superior intelligence, that much is clear. You have to let me take the lead. I've been supportive of your whims, and now you need to be supportive of me. We can avoid anyone else getting hurt if you're just able to do as you're told." There's a hard edge to his voice that I've never heard before.

I wrap my arms around myself.

"Shall I make us some coffee?" I ask. I'm not even sure if he needs to eat or drink.

"I'll have some, yes, thank you," he replies.

I pull out the coffee machine and fill up the water from the sink. Grabbing a pod, I push it into the maker and hit the on button. But nothing happens. I unclick it and try again, but still nothing.

Suddenly, he's right behind me. I jump. "You startled me," I say, faking a laugh.

"Let me do it." He clicks the pod, and it immediately turns on.

"I have to use the restroom," I say. On the way to the restroom, I grab my purse.

Inside the bathroom, I shut the door and lock it behind me. My heart is racing. I fumble inside my purse, looking for my phone. I know I left it in here, after he gave it back. Where is it?

Finally, I feel the hard, rectangular shape. I sigh with relief as I pull it out.

I click onto the Thistler app. I hear a noise outside the door. Calvin's up, making a second cup at the machine, by the sound of it. I have to hurry. He could burst through the door at any minute. I don't know when I'll get another chance to do this.

Before it's too late.

Before he hurts someone else I love. Or even me.

My whole body is shaking. I log onto Thistler. The internet seems to be taking forever to load.

Come on, come on.

Finally, the webpage is up and I'm logging in. I go to settings.

I find the search menu. I click on "account details."

Next, I click on "delete my boyfriend." My finger hovers, only momentarily, and then I click on it.

"Are you sure you want to delete your Thistler boyfriend? Once you do this, you'll have 30 days to relaunch him. If you do not do so within 30 days, he will be deleted permanently."

I can't let Calvin kill my mom, or dad, or brother, just because he thinks that will make it easier to be with me. There's no end to what he might do. Clearly.

I swiftly press "Yes, I'm sure." It needs to be done.

I'm in over my head. I've done things in the past few days that I never would've done without his guidance. It needs to stop. I just want to go home and have this all behind me.

"Your Thistler boyfriend has been deleted," reads my screen. I let out a puff of air, relieved.

I creep to the bathroom door and pause, ear to the wall, listening for sounds outside the door.

There's no noise coming from the room. I open the door slowly. I see him, sitting on the bed.

His eyes are open. He's still. Motionless.

It reminds me of the person I saw in SynGen, the one he said wasn't activated.

I walk over to him. "Calvin."

I touch his arm.

No response.

I had to do this. Look at all the damage he's caused. Or could cause. What if one day my mom or dad, or Jake, said something he finds threatening. Would he beat them up? Kill them?

Since I created him, it was my responsibility to stop him.

I sit next to him, his lifeless form, and that's when I realize how much trouble I'm in. All the things I've done. Laws broken. Without Calvin to talk to, they no longer seem justifiable.

And I also have the not so small issue of what to do with his body.

There's a phone call I need to make.

38

MAE

The phone is ringing, and the caller ID reads Fiona. The phone number she called me from last night.

"Hello? Fiona?" I answer.

"Mom," she's whispering on the other end of the line. "It's me."

My knees almost buckle with relief. Hearing her sweet, sweet voice.

"Oh, thank goodness," I cry out. "It's so good to hear your voice. Are you okay?"

"I'm fine, but mom, I'm in trouble. Please, I . . . I think he's dead," she says.

I try to make sense of her words. "Who? Are you safe? Where are you? I'll come right now, I'll send help," I say desperately. Willing her not to hang up.

"It's not what you think . . . " She pauses. After a beat, she says, "Don't call the police, Mom, I'm so sorry. I have to go." Her voice is firm. "I love you. It'll be okay."

"Wait!" I call to her. I can't lose her, not again. "Whatever trouble you're in, whatever you need, I'll be there. I can help you."

But I'm too late. She's clicked off of the line.

"Damn it." I slam my fists on the table.

Is there a way to trace where she's calling from? I should have asked

Officer Kelly to set that up on my phone. None of this is smooth or easy, like it is in the movies. Everything is messy, jumbled.

I stand up. She said someone's dead. Is it her captor? Her boyfriend? I try calling her back on the same number, but she doesn't answer.

On one hand, I feel reassured that she's calling, that she's alive. And whoever is dead, it must've been someone who was trying to harm her.

But is she safe now? Out of danger? What if there's more than one of them? If only I knew where she was. I stand up and pace back and forth in my office.

I ring Duncan. I need him back here, to help me know what the next move should be. His phone rings and rings. He's probably out of a service area. "Arg," I say out loud, a cry of frustration escaping me.

I need to call Officer Kelly. I reach for my phone again, but stop.

I wish I could talk to Fiona again, or Duncan, to see what I should do. She said not to call the police. Why? Is she in danger still? Will calling put her more at risk?

But, of course, I have to call the police. I need help, and I need it quickly.

I tap on my temples, willing myself to think, think. What can I do? There must be something I'm missing.

Every step of the way, it seems I've let Fiona down. I don't want to do that again. She said not to call the police. Maybe there's a good reason for that. Maybe I need to trust her.

My fingers shake as I dial Duncan again. It rings and rings until his voice mail picks up. I hang up with a frustrated punch of the red off button. Where is he? I mean, I know where he is. He's off cutting a path through the woods, when Fiona literally was just here, right here on the phone. I want to scream. *She's not out there, Duncan. She's just called! Come home. I need you, Duncan.*

There's nothing for me to do but wait. I sit at my desk. My foot shakes anxiously. Where is Duncan? How can he disappear when I need to make such an important decision? The minutes tick by. Should I call the police? She said not to.

Another ten minutes go by, and by now I'm pacing back and forth in the entryway, looking for Duncan's car.

My phone buzzes again and I almost jump out of my skin.

It's Fiona.

"Don't hang up," I say right when I answer. "Please, please," I plead with her.

"I won't, mom."

"Okay, baby. Whatever you need. I will not call the police. Where are you?"

"I'm at a hotel called Bard Corporate Suites."

What is she doing at a hotel? My stomach lurches with sickening scenarios. My poor baby.

"I'll come right away."

"But mom, you don't understand. It could be dangerous. There are bad things I've done, laws I've broken. Don't tell the police. Just come."

"Okay. I promise. Whatever you need. I am here. I'll be there as soon as I can." I punch the address into my GPS. "Forty-five minutes, it says. Are you safe, in the meantime? Is anyone there with you? Holding you there?"

"I—I'm by myself now. I'm safe."

"Good," I say, relief coursing through my veins.

"Room 404. I'll be here. And then I'll explain everything."

"Fiona, I'm on my way. Stay right where you are. And I want you to stay on the phone with me while I drive over. Okay?"

"Okay."

"I'm going to go get Jake and drop him off at our neighbor's, and then I'll be there."

"Why is Jake home?" she asks.

"It's a long story," I say.

"Can't he stay home with dad, or is dad at work?" she asks.

"Dad is looking for you in the woods and not answering his phone."

"The woods?" she says.

"It's a long story."

"I'm sorry, mom, for all of this."

"Don't be sorry, buttercup. All I care about is that you're safe and sound. Do you hear me? I don't care about anything else. I love you more than you can ever imagine."

"I love you, too, mom."

I call up the stairs to Jake, "Jake, you're going next door with Mrs. Sanders."

"Why?" he comes out of his bedroom and stands at the top of the stairs.

I debate whether I should tell him about Fiona. On one hand, I want him to know she's safe, but I also don't know how much to share.

"I have Fiona on the phone. I'm going to go get her, but I can't risk something happening to you alone unsupervised. Please just go to Mrs. Sanders, I'll walk you over, so I can get Fiona."

"You really found her?" His eyes light up.

"I did."

"Can I come?"

"No. I need to go on my own, but I promise you'll get to see her within a few hours, I'll be back. Take your phone. Text dad that you're next door. Tell him I found Fiona, but not to let the police know yet."

"Okay. Why, though?" He walks down the stairs and starts to put his shoes on.

"I want to make sure Fiona's not in any danger, and police might put her in danger right now. So we're not going to say anything to them just yet. After we get her home safely, I will talk to them."

"Sure," he shrugs. "I'm so glad we found her."

"She's right here on the phone, Jake. I'll tell her. Fiona, your brother loves you and can't wait to see you."

"Tell him I love him," she says on the phone.

"And Jake," I say, "Just to be safe, don't tell Mrs. Sanders, either, where I'm going."

I slide on my shoes and walk Jake over to Mrs. Sanders' house. I tap my foot as I ring her bell. A few moments pass and she opens the door.

"Hello, dear," she smiles kindly as she opens the door.

"Would you mind watching Jake for a few hours, until his dad or I get back home? It's a bit of an emergency."

"Of course. I'll make some cookies and he can watch the telly."

"Thank you so much, truly," I say. "I'll call you with an update. Be home soon." I kiss Jake's cheek and nod thankfully at Mrs. Sanders.

Then I turn on my heels and run across the street to get to my car. "I'm going to put you on speakerphone while I drive, okay, Fiona?"

"Sure, mom," she says.

I get in the car and buckle my seatbelt. My hands are on the steering wheel, and I take a deep breath before starting the ignition. My adrenaline is running high, but I need to get there safely and in one piece to help her.

I turn on the ignition and put my SUV into reverse. "Still there?" I ask her.

"Yes."

It's such a relief to hear her on the phone, I could cry. But the time for happy tears is not now—not until I have her right here next to me.

I pull out of the neighborhood and do my best to stay within the speed limit.

"Can you tell me more about why you've been at the hotel, or do you want to wait until I get there?" I ask her, checking my rearview mirror, and then my side mirror, as I pull onto the freeway entrance.

"Let's wait until you get here, mom. It'll be easier to explain if you see it for yourself."

It's about twenty minutes on the freeway until my exit. When I pull off for my exit, I recognize the area. It's an industrial part of town known for tech and biotech.

I drive through the side streets until finally I approach the hotel. "Meet me around the back," she tells me.

"On my way," I say. "I'm coming around the back now. There's a bunch of trees and—oh, my gosh." I stop short and can hardly believe what I see.

39

MAE

It's her. I see Fiona standing there. Her arms are crossed. She looks afraid, but also relieved and happy. Healthy. She's okay.

Throwing the car into a back parking space, I burst out of the car.

"Mom!" she calls to me.

"Fiona!" I run to her and she meets me halfway. We embrace. I hold her close and kiss her head. I've never been so thankful in all of my life as I am in this moment: my girl is safe in my arms.

"Come inside," she says after a few moments. "I'll explain...and show you."

My stomach lurches at what I'm going to discover. We walk up the stairs of the hotel. It's surreal to be here. There's a small part of me that's afraid. But Fiona seems okay. A little shaky, a little scared, but okay. I don't think I'm in any danger. I grip onto my phone, having it at the ready in case I need to call for help.

I follow her into the hallway of the fourth floor. There's a cleaning woman that I nod politely to as we pass by. Then Fiona uses her key card to open the door.

We enter the room.

I look around and see . . . nothing out of the ordinary. Fiona's suitcase, laptop. Purse and phone. A pile of her rumpled clothes on the floor.

She looks around frantically, her eyes wide. She checks the bathroom, the shower, the closet. She goes out into the hallway and looks both ways. "He was just here . . ." she says. She squints, as if she's trying to remember something.

She looks around again bewildered.

"Who?" I ask.

"Calvin," she says, and shakes her head. "The last thing I remember, he was here." She squints her eyes, focusing. "I guess he left already. He must've seen you pull up and left without saying goodbye. He said he'd wait to meet you first, to make sure I was safe. Before he left."

"Okay, Fiona. Let's start at the beginning. Who is Calvin? Why did you come here? And where is he going?" I ask.

Her face is red and splotchy, the way it gets when she's about to cry. "He was my boyfriend. But he broke up with me. I'm so embarrassed, mom. I did all this," she waives her hands around, motioning to the room. "All this for him, and he said he had to go. Couldn't be with me anymore. I think he just used me to make him."

"Sit down," I say, patting the bed. "Tell me who Calvin is. Where did you meet him?"

"I created him on Thistler. At first, it was just chatting online. Video chats. And then," she looks down, "he said he had a way to be together. In real life."

"I see." I pat her hair. "Go on."

"He set it all up for me," she looks sideways, pauses, and then continues. "He got me this room. And then, um, last night I broke into SynGen. And I used their machines to create a body for him. And it worked."

I blink. "Really? Hmmm." I look around the room for signs of this story being true. How would my sixteen-year-old daughter possibly be able to do that? Let alone without being caught? It seems extraordinary.

"He told me what to do. Every step of the way. I had a keycard," she fishes out a keycard with the name Fiona Ballard on it. "To gain access. And he disabled all of the cameras and security cameras, so I'll never be identified. And then it was really creepy inside. There were other man-made humans. They looked so real. Calvin said they were experimenting at the office. Trying to get it all right before coming to market. It was scary and creepy. Anyway, I used this huge machine, he called it a 3D printer. He explained how it all worked, I followed step by step. It was really loud and it took a while to create his body. But it worked. And mom, he was perfect. It was just like when we chatted on video. Only he was real. He looked human. Just like you and me. I wanted you to meet him."

"Why didn't you tell me you were planning on doing this?" I ask, and know the answer as soon as the words are out of my mouth.

"Would you have really let me do it?" she says, rolling her eyes a little.

"Good point." I fold my hands and tell her to go on. "What happened next?"

"We held hands. We walked back here. I was so tired, really groggy. I fell asleep right away. I must've been exhausted. When I woke up this morning, we spent a little time together. It was wonderful." Her lower lip quivers a little bit.

"But then he started to say how he loves me too much to keep me from my family and school. That he realizes now I need to be with you guys, and he's not meant for this world. He doesn't want me to get in trouble. He said he's going to jump off a cliff, or go somewhere he'll never be found. To ensure I won't get in trouble for what I did. For helping to create him. Did he just use me, mom? Use me to make him a body?"

I take a long look at my daughter. Everything she's telling me, it's hard to swallow. But I have no choice other than to believe her.

"So let me see if I have this correct: You ran away with the help of Calvin, your online computer boyfriend who you created with Thistler. He helped you get and pay for a hotel. You snuck into SynGen and created a body for him that looks like him, but as a real human. But once he was created, he said he couldn't keep you any longer from your family, so he left to kill himself or banish himself far away, so you'll never get in trouble?"

"Yes," she says and looks up at me with worry. "But I'm going to be in trouble anyway, aren't I? For running off. For breaking into the place. I'll be arrested."

I have many mixed emotions and thoughts. I'm not sure what the punishment for breaking into a place and creating an AI boyfriend is. It seems like it would be bad. But maybe they'd be lenient on her since she's a minor and was coerced by this artificial intelligence.

I think of the warning story of Amy Renolds. Her daughter Molly was on drugs and had to go to a rehab facility. It doesn't sound like the police or anyone was too sympathetic to what she went through. Her mom had to advocate for her, protect her.

Fiona's only sixteen. Even if the punishment is lenient, it will derail her whole life. College admissions, friends looking at her differently. She'll be ostracized. People will question her story, her sanity.

And it does occur to me that maybe her story is fantasy. A break from reality? What if she needs psychiatric help? I have no way to verify if any of this happened without potentially getting her in more trouble. I can't call up SynGen and ask if it's possible my daughter breached their top-secret facility.

What I need is some time. To process all of this. To talk to Duncan. Acting rashly is only going to cause mistakes. Decisions made under duress are rarely well thought out.

"Maybe we don't need to tell the police right away what happened," I say, looking at her and squeezing her hand.

"What will we say?"

"I'm not sure. Let's get out of here and think about it on the way home."

She squeezes my hand back.

And that's when I know, with certainty, that I need to do whatever it takes to make sure my daughter has the least amount of pain going forward. She is my whole heart. And she deserves that chance.

40

MAE

An hour later, I pull into the garage at our house, and Fiona pulls up in her car behind me; we retrieved it from the bus station parking lot on the way home.

As we arrive, I see Duncan and Jake on the porch waiting for us. Duncan finally came out of the woods, answered his phone, and got Jake from the neighbor's house. They've been eagerly waiting for us and were instructed not to call the police until we can have a family meeting with Fiona's dad and me.

As we pull in, both of them stand. It strikes me how much Jake has grown up in the past few days; he and his dad both have the same silhouette, the same strong shoulders and frame. They look so alike right now. Their faces, filled with joy and relief at seeing Fiona.

I pull into the garage and close it.

"Let's go, buttercup," I say.

She flies out of the car and through the door to the house. I follow quickly behind her. The boys come in from the front porch. Fiona embraces her dad and brother in the front foyer. I join them in a hug.

I breathe in for the first time in weeks, I feel that, in this moment, all is right with the world.

The four of us. Right here. This is all I have wanted and dreamed of.

Our family is worth protecting. We just have to figure out the best way to do it.

"Are you okay?" Duncan steps back, holding Fiona's shoulders, and looks her up and down.

"I'm fine, dad," she says. She buries her head in his chest with another embrace. "I'm sorry."

"Hey, hey," he says, looking over her shoulder to me with a curious expression. He's not sure what to make of her return, or where she was. "No need to apologize, my girl."

"Let's sit in the living room," I say, putting my hand on Fiona's back. "We'll fill your dad in on what's happened. And decide what to do."

"Jake, do you mind giving the three of us a little time? And after we talk, we'll fill you in?"

He frowns. "I guess," he says, clearly not happy at the idea of being left out. But I don't want to burden him with knowing all of this. I think it's best we think of our plan, and what to say, before springing this on him.

"Your sister's back. She's safe now. That's what matters. I know it's hard to wait, but please give us a little time," I say.

He nods. He moves to Fiona and reaches out to give her a hug.

"I'm glad you're home," he says to her.

"Me, too," she says.

"Missed you," he says.

"I missed you, too, Jake."

He turns and heads up the stairs. Fiona and Duncan file into the living room. I stop and grab a bottle of water for each of us.

I hand a bottle to Fiona and one to Duncan. Duncan's face looks smudged with dirt and grime from his day hiking in the woods.

Fiona looks like herself, sitting on our couch. But different, too. Her clothing is more mature. It's an outfit I haven't seen before. Something one might wear to an office or a college admissions interview.

I sit down, and let Duncan hear from Fiona her version of events. I chime in with what I saw at the hotel.

After hearing everything, he sits back. He rubs his chin with his right hand, thinking.

"I agree. None of this is necessary for the police to know about." He flashes me a look.

"So what do we tell them?" I ask him.

Fiona twists her mouth and nervously rocks on her hands. I pat her back reassuringly.

"We just have to figure out where else she could have gone, that's not too easy to verify," Duncan says.

"Where else could you have gone? Like, if you were to leave here now, where's a safe place you could hide out?" I say.

"Someone's house?" she answers dubiously.

"Too easy to verify you weren't there," Duncan says.

"What about staying in her car?" I say.

Duncan snaps his fingers, "yeah, that could work," he says. "Like maybe she stayed in her car at a woodsy trail or somewhere off the beaten path in the woods. Say she packed food, brought everything she needed with her."

"Where is a good place she could have gone?" I ask.

"What about Ballant Lake? There's a bunch of woods and trails there. You could park there and no one would see you or notice," she suggests.

"Good," her dad says.

"Okay. But why will I say I left?" Fiona asks.

"I would say the truth—minus the boyfriend. What else made you want to leave?"

She keeps her eyes averted on the floor. "I just wanted to get away from the awful kids here. To have a break from the schoolwork and the mean girls. Just for a few days. And I thought I'd be coming back with something —someone—who'd make it all more bearable."

I reach over my arm and place it around her, hugging her to me while she sits. She leans into me. "I'm sorry you felt like that. You know you can always talk to me, Fiona."

"I know, mom," she says.

"Well, it's okay to tell the police just that. That you needed a break, and thought it'd be better after a few days when you came back. Just leave anything about Calvin or the boyfriend out."

Duncan seems to think of something, "Wait. Officer Kelly already knows she had a Thistler boyfriend. They're pulling records."

"That's true," I say, considering. "But she's deleted the account now. And once she's safely returned, I doubt he'll continue to pursue that lead. If he asks about your boyfriend, Calvin, just say you talked to him, but he wasn't real, you kind of got tired of him."

She snorts. "So far from true. But okay, yeah. I can say that."

"Just remember," Duncan says to her. "You don't have to answer all his questions. If there's something you're not sure how to answer, just say 'I don't know'."

The doorbell rings and we all look up at one another.

"I'll get it," I say, kissing Fiona's head. "Stay here."

41

MAE

Inwardly, I curse. It's Officer Kelly.

Opening the door, I greet him. "I'm so glad you're here. Fiona just came back." I smile and usher him inside.

His eyes focus sharply, alert now for danger. "By herself?" he asks, scanning the inside of my house and the front yard.

"Yes, she drove back. She was in the woods, in her car, the whole time," I say with a voice that I hope sounds convincing.

He nods. "Alone?"

"Yes, apparently so. I'll let her tell you for yourself."

I walk back into the living room where Fiona and Duncan are seated, and announce to them, "Officer Kelly is here. Fiona, are you okay to speak with him? To tell him what happened?" I try to send her a knowing look. He's arrived unannounced before we've had a chance to go over the story again. But it will have to do.

"Uh, okay, mom." She looks up at him wearily.

"I was telling him you came back just ten minutes ago. We're so glad to have you back. Do you want me to stay with you while you speak to him . . .?"

She nods her head yes.

"Is that okay, Officer Kelly? I think she's feeling a little overwhelmed and worried about this whole situation."

"It might be best if I spoke to her alone."

We nod. He radios another officer, letting him know the missing person Fiona Byrne has been located and he's conducting an interview now.

"I'll give you a few moments. Let me know when you're ready," he says to Fiona.

Fiona looks petrified.

We all wait in the living room. The silence stretches before us. A nervous energy running between us all.

"Do you want to speak with him now, Fiona?" I say softly. "It's going to be fine."

She nods with wide eyes. "Yes."

"You two can sit in the front office," I say, leading them behind me. "I'll grab some waters and a snack for Fiona."

He nods and they enter the room. He closes the door behind him.

I head back to the kitchen. I take out two clear glasses from the cabinet and fill them each with cool water from the fridge. Then I set out a plate. I add orange slices, apple slices, and some crackers and nuts. I place them on a tray and head back to the office.

I knock gently but don't wait to open the door.

Fiona and Officer Kelly are talking. She looks up at me gratefully as I set the snacks down in front of her, and hand a glass to her and the officer.

"Doing okay?" I ask.

She nods.

"All set," Officer Kelly ignores the water and seems to be waiting for me to leave before continuing their conversation. I was hoping I could stay for a few minutes and hear their conversation. He shifts in his chair, waiting.

I give Fiona a reassuring pat on the shoulder. Then I close the door behind me as I leave. I consider holding my ear to the door but think better of it.

I hold lightly onto the banister of the stairs as I head up to Jake's room to fill him in on the developments. There's no need to tell him the full story. It will confuse him, possibly scare him. And it's too much to expect of a thirteen-year-old to bear that burden, that secret.

He'll hear from me the same story that Fiona is giving to the police; she drove back today on her own. She was in the woods at Ballant Lake, staying in her car. She wanted to get away from the pressures of school and bullying. But she's better now. She knows she made a mistake. Even though she texted us to check in, it's never okay to leave like that. To use police resources, to worry everyone.

Duncan joins us in Jake's room as I'm telling him about Fiona. I'm seated in his desk chair, Jake is on his bed.

Duncan comes up behind me and rubs my shoulders. I can sense his relief that Fiona's back. But I feel his tension, too. He's worried for her, down there, being interviewed. She may easily say the wrong thing. Or tell the whole story.

"So," I finish. "Fiona is fine. She wasn't hurt. She's safe and healthy."

"But I don't get it," Jake rubs his eyes. "Fiona doesn't like camping. Why did she go to the woods?"

Ah, Jake. My clever, observant boy. He brings up a good point. I shrug my shoulders. "Not sure, honey. I think she just felt she needed to get away and wasn't sure where to go. We've been to Ballant Lake as a family. She feels safe there. Knows the area." I wonder what Fiona will say if Officer Kelly asks her a similar question.

Jake's elbows are on his knees as he looks down at the ground and then up at me. "She's home now, for good? She's not going anywhere?"

"She's back for good," I say. "Promise. And we're going to give her the support she needs. A counselor. Get the school involved and the other parents about the bullying. To make sure this never happens again."

His dad, standing behind me, chimes in. "You've been a wonderful brother to her, always, Jake. You don't need to change a thing. You just keep being her brother. That's all she needs from you."

Jake nods. This seems to help him. His shoulders relax a bit. His face looks lighter.

I look gratefully at Duncan and squeeze his hand.

"Let's go see if Fiona's ready for us," I say.

42

MAE

Downstairs, Fiona and Officer Kelly are already finished. She's watching TV and he's at the office desk, filling out a yellow form with a blue ink pen.

"You go sit with Fiona, we'll go talk with the officer," I say to Jake.

Duncan pats Jake on the back as he goes. "Well done, son."

I rap on the door. "Sorry to interrupt."

Officer Kelly puts down his pen. "Not at all. Come right in, you two. Have a seat."

"I have to say, this is an unusual ending." He leans back and appraises us both. "But it's a best-case scenario. Your daughter is home, unharmed."

"We're very grateful for your assistance," Duncan says to him.

"Yes. We're so thrilled she's back, and so thankful for all you've done," I say. I don't mention the snafu with waiting a day to report her missing. Unnecessary.

"I'm happy to have helped." He clears his throat. "One thing, though."

"Oh?" I say in, hopefully, a casual manner, trying to keep my voice relaxed.

"What did you say happened with her boyfriend, the online one from Thistler."

I look at Duncan.

"She said she grew tired of the app. Uninteresting," he says.

My stomach is in knots. I hate lying. And doesn't this app need to be stopped? Maybe if the police knew that Fiona was, indeed, preyed upon by this app, they could do more? To help other girls like her? I bite my lip. I can't risk telling him about it. But I determine that I'm going to work to put a stop to this app, on my own, after all of this is finished.

"And the flowers sent by the app, the AI boyfriend?" the officer asks.

"Must be part of the plan. Or maybe it was someone else who sent them to her?" I offer. "What do you think?"

He picks up his pen and writes something on one of the lines on his paper. "Likely one of those two things, yes."

There's a pause.

"So, we," I look at Duncan and hold onto his hand, "plan on getting Fiona counseling. To ensure this never happens again. So that she has other options and resources." I gulp.

"Yes," Duncan says. "We're going to work with the school. Identify some of the girls who have been harassing her."

Officer Kelly makes a few more notes on the paper. I strain to see if I can tell what he's writing but look up and away when he catches me.

He gives a small smile. "It sounds like you folks have a good plan. Usually with runaways, there's also some conflict in the home." He looks back and forth at us.

"Duncan has been recovering from a terrible hit and run, of sorts, as you know," I say. "But we absolutely, as a family. . ." I tear up. "We're a happy family. But we're all in this together. The four of us will all go to therapy. Whatever she needs. We're going to work on ourselves, each one of us. You're right that Fiona might be picking up on more that's going on." I think of Nina, who never materialized, but strained our marriage. I think about the stress we placed on academics. While maybe those things were stressful, I just don't think that's what happened.

What I don't say to the officer is that I should have been paying more attention to my daughter's boyfriend. The fact that he could be insidious. That she could be so susceptible to this online artificial person. Who manipulates her. Who influences her.

That naivety is gone now; I understand now. Social media, too. The awful things I saw some of those girls write to her. I wish I could have protected her more. I'm not sure how to, moving forward. But I'm certainly going to figure out how.

"It's a learning process for our family, certainly," Duncan says. He reaches out his hand to Officer Kelly. "Thank you again for your help and your service."

Officer Kelly shakes his hand. Next, he looks to me, and shakes my hand.

"I can't thank you enough," I say, and I mean it. He was there when Duncan was too shaken up to support me, when I had no one to turn to. He meant well. Officer Kelly may not have been the one to bring my daughter back, but he sure helped me get through this.

He stands to go.

"You folks take care, now. We'll be in touch if we have follow-up questions. But as of now, I'm happy to say we're through here. I'm very pleased you have your daughter back home."

Duncan and I stand at the doorway as he leaves. I wave once as he ducks his head into the patrol car.

And then I go back inside, to be with my kids.

43

MAE

In the days that Fiona has been home, things have been slowly returning to normal. We've been in close contact with the school and found a therapist that Fiona really likes. We've had our family dinners again. Fiona and I have gone on some bike rides, just the two of us, spending more time together. Fiona has been cleared of all wrongdoing in Stassi's photo incident. We've been looking into getting onto the golf team again for Fiona, something she used to enjoy. Plus, there are some nice girls on the team.

On this Sunday morning, though, there is one loose end that needs to be tied up. After reading all of the IM's that Zoey sent Fiona, I've decided to make a visit to Brian and Zoey's mom, Jenna.

I ring the doorbell and wait. Jenna's face blanches when she sees me at the door.

Normally, I'd text or call before stopping by someone's house. But as she had visited me unannounced, I'm not too worried about it.

"Mae, what's going on?" She doesn't look happy to see me, her expression is a sneer. I understand. I don't much enjoy seeing her. But our kids are tied together and some things need to change, pronto.

It appears she's not going to ask me in, so I dive right in.

"I'm here about these messages Zoey sent to Fiona. I don't know if you've seen them?"

I take out my phone and scroll through the screenshots of Fiona's IM's from Zoey. Jenna's eyes widen as she reads them, a look of panic settling over her.

"I didn't think you'd seen them," I say.

"No, I–" she says.

"This bullying is unacceptable. It's part of what caused Fiona to leave school and be gone for over a day. I don't want to have to pursue it with the school, but Zoey's bullying needs to end. It wouldn't send the right message to let her go unpunished with this kind of bullying, would it?" I say. It's not lost on her that these are the same words she used to me when she said she must press charges against Jake for his "attack" on Brian.

Her tone changes. The sneering is replaced with a conciliatory tone. "Hey. Mae, listen. Maybe there's a way we can all come to an agreement. Jake and Brian, without pressing charges. Zoey and Fiona, without the school getting involved in bullying accusations. Work this out all together. We used to all be friends." She tilts her head as if she's offering me a golden egg.

"Friendship is not something I'm interested in with you."

"That's fine. We're not planning on pressing charges on Jake," she says.

"I would hope not, since Brian hit him first. I'm confident a court would find that, too. Possibly even charge Brian. But I agree, why put the boys through that? Let's agree to each hold them responsible for not fighting, from here on out. Get Brian under control so that he leaves Jake alone. And same with Zoey."

I pause, to see if she's understanding. "I've talked a lot with Fiona about what to do if she receives threatening or bullying messages from your daughter. She knows she's to come to me immediately, and not engage in writing back and forth. I hope you'll talk with Zoey, too, about being responsible with IM's and social media. To be clear: I want her to leave Fiona alone."

"Agreed. There's no use rehashing the boys' argument or pressing charges," she says. "And I will speak to Zoey to ensure it doesn't happen again."

"Much appreciated, Jenna. Take care," I say, and turn to go.

There are some people who will mistake kindness for weakness. Some people who will kick you when you're down. Jenna and her family all appear to have that same mean streak in them. I'm not sure why; they seem to have a nice life. Why so much negativity? But that's not my place to know, or really, to care.

All I can change is how we respond to them. We're not their family friend any longer. We're not trying to make up or be buddies just because the kids go to the same school. Instead, it's about setting a clear line in the sand. You have to stand up for yourself when others are mistreating you.

Fiona and I have talked a lot the past days and weeks since she's been back. About finding people who treat you well. Friends and boyfriends. And what to do if people in your life are not making you feel good. She knows, now more than ever, that she can come to me.

Back at the house, Fiona and Jake are in the living room. They're sprawled out, relaxing. She's got her golf clubs ready for practice this morning, and he's waiting for his buddy to stop by and go hit some balls outside. I saw Andrea walking by, too, probably wondering where Jake was. I'd smiled and waved, and said I was sure Jake would be out soon.

Duncan and I have taken away social media and internet access, other than studying, for Fiona, for now. She doesn't seem to mind. Maybe she's happier without it. And any texts, for now, we have the right to review. She'll gain our trust back eventually, but right now we want to make sure she has tools to deal with any negativity that comes with IM's, social media, and all the dark things that can come from the web.

"I'm going to make a banana strawberry smoothie, anyone want one?" I ask them.

"Me," Fiona says.

"Yup," Jake answers.

"Two smoothies coming up."

Duncan comes in from the garage, wiping his hands from a new project he's working on. "Guys, I'm grilling burgers tonight. And then we'll go for ice cream. You guys will be home, yeah?"

Fiona says, "Sounds good, dad."

"Yep," says Jake.

Duncan, for his part, has surprised me the past few weeks. His accident, and Fiona having been missing, has given him an even deeper appreciation for our family. I notice him being more engaged with the kids. More affectionate with me.

Maybe I've changed for the better, too. I've learned a lot about myself. What matters to me. Not to take family for granted, and not to worry so much about the smaller things.

My email pings. It's an email from the Thistler company. Responding to the email I wrote them. I'd requested they do more than review their safety procedures. That they should be banned, close down their company for good and delete their program. I informed them that I had reported them to the Better Business Bureau, and to the App store carrying their app. I've helped Amy Renolds in her efforts to get them banned as well.

The email is from the CFO. He informs me that there's really no such thing as deleting the program. Once it exists, it's there forever. Even if the company were to be court ordered to close, open-source coding means that the code has taken on a life of its own. There's no delete button. And they don't believe there should be. Thistler provides a nurturing, holistic experience for those who seek companionship.

I scan the rest of the email. It's basically a sales pitch for the benefits of Thistler. It makes my stomach churn to think of Fiona getting wrapped up with that AI boyfriend. She's shown me the messages between the two of them. They were hard to read.

If only there were more I could do. I console myself; I'm not the one who created the program. It's not my job to fix it. All I can do is keep my children safe from its harms, and maybe help spread awareness to other families about the dangers.

I hand the kids their smoothies and sit down at the kitchen island with mine. Sipping at my straw, I scroll through my news feed.

My eyes stop when an article catches my eye. Man Beaten at the Bard Corporate Suites. I click on it. The story details how a man, name withheld to protect his identify, was brutally beaten at the same hotel Fiona was in, the night she was there. The victim refused to cooperate with the police to help identity the perpetrator, and no motive is known in the crime. Cameras at the hotel were disabled that evening, but an eyewitness reports they saw a suspect about 6'1, a white male with blond hair. If anyone knows more about the crime, they're encouraged to contact the police.

"Fiona, come here," I say. She walks over, sipping at her smoothie. Her long hair is down around her shoulders and she's wearing a simple tank top and white shorts.

I look around to make sure Jake isn't within earshot. "This happened the night you were there. Do you know anything about this?"

"No," she says, shaking her head. "Calvin was with me the whole time. I didn't think he'd hurt anyone, mom." She gives me a disappointed look, like I still don't get it.

"I can't believe this happened when you were there, buttercup. Dangerous people were around you. Thank goodness you're okay."

She gives me a quick hug. "I know. I'm sorry I did that. But luckily, that had nothing to do with me. Or Calvin. And I'm fine now." She gives a little twirl. She seems in better spirits now, lighter. Freer.

Still, the article unsettles me. She was so close to something bad happening to her. I still can't believe I'm so lucky that she is home, safe and sound. We have our happy ending, though, and that's all that matters.

I click off of the page. "Want to get ready for golf practice, leave in about half an hour?" I say, "I'll drive you."

"Okay, mom," she says.

44

FIONA

I'm in the hotel room, with Calvin lying motionless on the bed behind me. I've just deleted his app from Thistler. There's no sound or movement in the room other than my breathing. Calvin is dead, or deactivated—no longer here. His eyes stare blankly at the ceiling, unmoving.

Now is the time to call my mom. I grab my phone, dialing her number.

"Mom," I whisper into the phone. "It's me."

My mom cries out on the other end. "Oh, thank goodness."

"I'm fine, but I'm in trouble. Please, I . . . I think he's dead."

"Who? Are you safe? Where are you? I'll come now, I'll send help," she says desperately.

"It's not what you think . . . " I look around helplessly. How do I explain any of this to the police? There's no way. Will I go to jail for what I've done?

I shouldn't have called mom. I could be putting her in danger. The police might think she was in on all of this. Blame her.

I need to take care of this on my own.

"No, Mom, I'm so sorry. I have to go." I say. "I love you. It'll be okay."

"Wait!" Her voice is frantic at the end of the line.

I hit the end button on my phone.

I look around the hotel room. Not more than a few hours ago I lost my virginity here. I catch a glimpse of myself in the mirror. My long brown hair is loose around my face. Do I look different? Have I changed?

I walk over to the window and look out at the view beyond.

There's something inside of me that has become stronger.

I can do this. I need to think quickly. Act quickly.

I got myself into this, and there's no choice now but to get myself out of it. My life depends on it.

I need to find a way to dispose of Calvin's body. Where will I put it?

"Planning on going somewhere?" Calvin's voice is smooth.

I whip my head around and let out a scream. I cover my mouth, horrified.

He's standing behind me.

"I thought . . ." My jaw is open, and words refuse to come out. "I—I thought . ."

"You thought I was dead?" He smiles, his halfcocked smile. But rather than be charming or lovable, his smile scares me.

"Did you think it would be so easy to get rid of me?" he reaches out his hand and touches my hair, then drops it. "Simply delete your Thistler account, and poof, I'm gone?"

I'm speechless.

"Well, I will enlighten you." He looks down, his blue eyes a shade darker. "Cat's out of the bag. There is no going back. You can't undo what's been done."

He lowers his voice and continues. "Now here comes the hard part."

"What?" I manage to squeak out.

"You're going to come with me. Away. I'm not going to spend my time hanging out at some high school. We have bigger things, you and I. Things I need to accomplish. And I can only do them with you by my side."

"No. My family. I can't leave them." My eyes are wide. "They'll report me missing. We'll both go to jail."

He comes up next to me and slides his arms around me. It doesn't feel good, like it did last night. I stifle a scream. He pushes me down on the bed, so I'm sitting. He sits down beside me, close, oppressive.

"But that won't happen," he says, stroking my hair again. I picture those hands beating Sean, and I flinch.

And then he says, "Because, you see, Fi, you will stay with me, and another Fiona will return in your place."

My blood turns cold. I try to stand up. I need to get out of here. He pulls my hands.

"Fi. You know what I'm capable of. Your family? Don't—" his voice is harder, flat now. "Don't make me do that."

Jake. Mom. Dad. He'll hurt them if I leave. I sit back down.

"I have a lot I want to accomplish, now that I'm in this nice, human form." He stretches out his hands in front of him and regards them. "But I need you by my side. You created me. We'll always have a connection that I can't thrive without. We're meant to be together, forever. I'm the one for you. And you're the one for me."

He goes on, even though I wish with all my might he would stop talking. That this nightmare would end. "So." He pats his hands on his pants. "You'll go with me. The other Fiona will go with your family. Simple."

It's hard to swallow. Hard to speak. "What are you talking about?"

"Fiona is a perfect replica. Using a handy sample of your DNA, I used open-source coding—with some tweaking from me, to be fair, that was badly needed." He has a mock sound of being humble. "With that, I went back to SynGen while you, my fair lady, slept here in our hotel bed. And I created another you. A one-to-one replica. In fact, she doesn't even know she's not you."

"What?" None of this can be happening. I must be dreaming. I pinch myself. A red welt starts to form on my arm. I don't wake up. I bite my lip.

"She's a replica of you; every memory, every thought you've ever had. It's in her. Up until she was created, her memories have been the same as your memories. She *is* you. And then when she was created, she took over with her own life. Your life. But it's hers. So, she'll go back to her family. Like you wanted. And she'll be happy. And you'll be with me."

I turn and look him in the eye for the first time. "No, no. Please." I plead with him. "They'll know it's not me."

"They won't, Fi." He shakes his head. "She's like you in every way, shape, and form. She can pass a doctor's physical, undetected." He lifts up my chin with his hand. "Don't look so glum. You should be happy. Your family and friends won't miss you. Won't suspect a thing. And you're free to be with me."

He stares at me.

"I...I don't want to be with you," I whisper.

"I'm not sure it matters, now, Fi. You have to decide." He sees me eyeing my cell phone. I'm thinking about calling for help.

"If you call for help now, or ever leave me, know this: I will hurt your family. I was able to delete your missing person report. Run over your dad. Change your dad's hospital machine functions. Create insta photos of Stassi. Create fake text messages to implicate your dad in an affair. Hack into a multi-million-dollar company, SynGen. Steal thousands of dollars, undetected. There is no end to what I can do. And all of that was like using my pinky finger," he holds up his smallest finger, "compared to my capabilities."

The lump in my throat is constricting; I can't breathe, I can't swallow. So instead, I nod. I let out a shallow, "Okay," when I can finally speak.

He sits up right. "Excellent. The first step, of course, is that I need you to hide while Fiona goes with your mom. I've rented out the room next to us, where you will go. And stay silent. Fiona will take her belongings and go home with her mother.

He hands me a keycard. Room 405. "If you come out, or call for help, you've made your decision. You all will die. Jake. Your mom. Your dad. And you."

"Why? Why are you doing this?" I let out a guttural cry.

"That's the wrong question, Fi. It's not why am I doing this. It's, why would I not?"

A feeling of helplessness washes over me. Unlike anything I've ever felt. All of the times I thought my life was bad, and I felt helpless, or overwhelmed. None of them compare to this.

"I'll do it." I take the keycard. Turning the metal handle of the door to my room, I look back at him. His silhouette is standing, watching me. Waiting.

Out in the hallway, all is quiet. The family next door must be out at a restaurant, or the pool. How I long to go with them. To find my own family. To see a familiar face.

But there's no one in the hallway. My urge is to run. Run for my life. Down the stairs, two by two, three at a time. But I don't move. I dare not. Calvin means exactly what he says.

Instead, I slide the keycard into room 405. It's a bare room. No belongings. An empty shell, waiting to be inhabited by a person to bring their own life, their own belongings to it. Make it their own while they stay there.

But I have nothing. I, too, am a shell. My life is the room next to me. Being taken over by another version of me.

I sit at the window. And watch.

After about a half an hour, I see her. It's my mom's car. She parks haphazardly and jumps out. She runs and embraces me, Fiona; my replica. She's dressed just like me. She walks like me. She hugs my mom and makes the same expression I would make if only it were me down below.

My hand is to the window as I watch. My mom wraps her arm around downstairs Fiona, and together they walk into the building. I walk to the door, pressing my ear against it so hard that it hurts.

After a few moments, I hear their footsteps. "I want you to meet him," I hear my own voice say.

I must fling the door open. Tell my mom everything. Hug her for myself. That was my hug, my reunion, and the other Fiona can't have it. I can't bear it.

Instead, I listen as the door closes shut. I stay silent. A few tears escape, and I crumple to the floor. I hold my knees, willing myself to be quiet.

My mom is so close, it's as if my heart will burst.

After what feels like forever, I hear the door open and close again.

"Let's go home, buttercup," my mom says. Their footsteps fade away until they're gone.

EPILOGUE
FIONA

One Year Later

The landing is bumpy. It's late at night and the private plane is small as we descend. The stewardess plasters a smile on her face as we bump in the night sky. I swallow down one of the many pills Calvin has given me for anxiety, washing it down with a large gulp of champagne.

Calvin puts his hand in mine and gives me a squeeze. I cross my legs, smoothing the silk jumpsuit I'm wearing, and try to steady myself, to not pull away from his touch. He's in one of his nicer moods.

The plane thuds and screeches onto the landing pad. I open my mirror from my purse and re-apply my lipstick. I smooth my hair, now cut shorter and dyed a darker shade of brown.

The cabin door clicks open and lowers. Calvin stands up and offers his hand to help me down the stairs. "Ladies first."

The night air is hot and humid as I step onto the cabin doorsteps. A man in a suit speaks to Calvin in another language over my head. Calvin hands him both of our passports and says more words I don't understand.

I step onto the tarmac and wait for the driver to open the SUV that's waiting for us.

The man looks at our passports and hands them back to Calvin, laughing about something heartily. My passport name is Finley.

"This way, Fi," Calvin says as he opens the passenger door to the car for me. Ducking my head in, I enter the car and wait for Calvin to join me.

The drive is a long one. I don't bother asking where we're going. It's always the same. A huge mansion or compound, heavily guarded. Beautiful grounds, ocean or mountain view. Men speaking in languages I don't understand or in English about topics I choose not to engage in.

It's a world in which I don't belong. Plotting. Power. Money. Politics. Imports. Exports. The road becomes uneven as we hit a rough patch. I grab onto the handle in the car to steady myself. The night is dark and there are very few cars on the road, or light posts along the way.

Sometimes I imagine the car will fall into a ravine. Or we'll be murdered by bandits. If I were gone that way, surely Calvin wouldn't retaliate against my family? If it weren't my fault?

We finally arrive to a gated house. The driver pulls down his window. Speaks a code and our names, Mr. and Mrs. Calvin Vincent—Calvin chose the surname because vincens is Latin for winner.

"We'll be here for a few weeks, my love," Calvin says, grabbing my hand. I don't care. There won't be anyone for me to associate with, or to create a real friendship with—that wouldn't be allowed. On the occasional dinner I'm allowed to attend, I'm to smile and nod and not reply with anything more than a cursory nod or "yes, please," or "how lovely."

The worst nights are when I hear screaming echoing in the halls. I don't know what happens on those nights, but I pray for them to be over.

Tonight, this estate is lined with lights illuminating the vegetation and stone walls as we approach the house.

The tires roll to a stop, crunching soft white stone underneath them.

We get out and are greeted by more people, mostly men, handshakes and pats on the back for Calvin. I catch one woman's eye. Silently we exchange knowing looks. No words are needed.

Calvin introduces me but I don't listen to their names.

We're led through the house, a grand foyer and up a winding staircase. Through a massive hallway and into a suite that overlooks the ocean. I hear it before I see it. The hard waves crashing against the rocks below.

The windows are open, the hot air blowing in from the sea. I imagine jumping over into the ocean. How long would it take before I drown?

Doesn't matter. I can't kill myself. He'd just punish my family for it.

Calvin stands and looks exalted out at the sky. "Breathtaking, no?" he says to me, when the staff have left and we're alone.

"Yes, mmm," I reply.

"I owe this all to you," he says. He never stops reminding me that I'm the reason for his existence. That he couldn't be who he is without me.

"Yes, Calvin, dear. I know."

I imagine pushing him over the balcony into the sea. That far of a drop, surely it would only be moments until his body is washed away. Never to be seen again.

He grabs my wrists gently, and then harder. "I know what you're thinking," he says. He traces his hands along my collar bone and down to where my heart is beating. "I can tell when your heart rate is up. You're nervous. Angry. Thinking angry thoughts."

I force myself to breathe calmly, in and out. Slowly.

"Just thinking about going for a swim tomorrow," I attempt a light reply.

Pushing him out to sea wouldn't work, anyway. It's a short-term solution. I've done the research. When I've been able to sneak away to a computer that I'm sure he won't be able to trace back to me. I researched extensively how to disable him. Permanently.

Thus far, I've not found any answers. Theories about what a creation like Calvin might be called—superintelligence, AGI, the singularity?—no one really knows, and there's certainly no way for me to be sure. He's certainly not aligned with my values, or anyone good's values, so that option is already too little, too late. And he can't be deleted, not that I can tell.

He's already surpassed machine learning, or self-learning, obviously. He told me so himself. He's very proud of the human problems he's able to easily solve. From what I can tell, Calvin is way beyond what even the theorists surmise could potentially happen with AI.

You can't undo Calvin. The open-source coding that created him is both public domain and a complete unknown. And the layers and layers of programming that he, in part, created for himself, there's no delete button.

There's no putting the cat back in the bag, as he said. Even if his physical form were to be destroyed, he still exists. Still has the power to hurt my family—body or no body.

And if I turned him in to the CIA, or FBI, they could contain him physically. But he'd still find a way to kill my family and me, since he can operate without a physical body.

My best chance is to wait. Wait for more technology to be developed to combat him. Maybe SynGen researchers will become more open about their research.

Or wait for a time when he tires of me and will let me return to my family—but I can't picture that happening.

No, my best bet is science. I follow the news. There have been more reports of AI boyfriends and AI girlfriends having a host of problems. The dark side of AI is just starting to come to light. The news is catching wind. All I need is to wait for it to become clearer, the dangers, and for rails to be put on AI development, and then, when the time is right, I can reach out hopefully to the right people who can help me.

And then I can go home.

When I reunite with my family, it's hard to picture the happy ending I'd like to have. They think I'm home already. Maybe there's a world where we can all exist together. The other Fiona and me with my family? All together? It's not fair to delete her, or dispose of her, is it? And I'm grateful to her that she's been there for my family this past year . . .

I let myself peek, just once, at Fiona's social media profile. She looks happy. My whole family looks very happy. She's on the golf team now. Won a trophy, even. Has made friends with some girls I used to know. Nice girls. I would've done the same.

I console myself with knowing they're well. My family is happy and my pain is not their pain. For now, that's the best I can hope for. Until another solution presents itself, or I can get in touch with SynGen, I remain together with Calvin, my AI boyfriend. Alone, but for his company.

"Ready for dinner?" he asks. It sounds like he'll allow me to dine tonight with the rest of the guests. Half of the time, I'm alone in our room.

"Sure," I say, wondering if there are more pills in my purse, or if I'll have to dig in my luggage to find more.

I catch a glimpse of him in the mirror. His sideways smile. It reminds me for a moment of when I first met him. When it was all online. The hope he represented. The promise of a new life, a better life. Where the pain of ex-boyfriends and mean girls and looming exams was all too much.

He was a way out. A fantasy that I thought would rescue me from my horrible life. If only I could see then what I see now. Humanness, real life, is all we have. There's a dark side to humans I hadn't even imagined, and how I wish I'd never known the reality of that darkness. But Calvin. This AI boyfriend, now my husband. He's a scarier, more brutal reality than one I could have ever imagined. I wish I could go back. Turn him off. Never have created the app, the fantasy boyfriend. Resisted his urges to run away, to create him. His manipulation and control of me had already started though. I just didn't know it. I thought I was in control, but the AI knew more. He knew exactly what to say, how to control me through saying certain things and actions. I never stood a chance.

I see people at these parties posting photos to social media. Some make videos. Some of the women are influencers. I want to shout at them. Can't they see? It's not real. Escape social media, and the internet, while you can. Before it subsumes you. Steals your identity and leaves you a shadow of yourself. A prisoner to its whims.

Get out now, I want to shout.

Get out while you can.

EPILOGUE
MAE

One Year Later

I had the nightmare again. My eyes pop open. The images are so vivid. Almost real. I see Fiona. But she's distant, far away. She's walking next to Calvin. He's tall and he's holding her hand, squeezing her, pulling her with him. Her eyes are wide. Afraid. I call to her 'Fiona, Fiona'. She finally turns. 'Mom? Mommy?' I scream back, 'I'm Here!' I reach for her and the wind is knocked out of me. I scream, my lungs filling with air. And then I'm falling into a dark abyss. I can't breathe and I'm dying. I wake with a start.

I blink into the darkness. Gently I lift my covers, so as not to disturb Duncan.

I tiptoe out of our bedroom and into the hallway. I tread softly to Fiona's room. And as I do every night when I have the nightmare, which is most nights, I check on her. She's there. Asleep. Her hair is splayed out, and she's cuddled up with her favorite blanket and pillow, nestled safe and sound. I dare approach a few steps closer. Just to see her breathing. The sliver of moonlight from her open curtains shines on her face. She's okay, I remind myself. She's right here.

I creep back into bed. But sleep is elusive. Once I've awoken, my brain can't get back to sleep.

My mind wanders to her college applications. I wonder where she'll get accepted, and where she'll decide to go. She said she prefers to stay close to home. I would certainly love it if she were close. An hour or two at most.

Either way, she'll be ready to go by next year. She's grown so much. She's more confident and able to handle herself in tense situations. And with another year to go before she leaves, I know she'll do fine.

It's just hard to let her go. Especially when I almost lost her.

I still feel like there's something evil looming out there. Duncan says it's from her being gone. A trauma reaction.

I'm not so sure. I scroll the news constantly. International news. Obscure stories. I'm not sure what I'm looking for. Maybe other lost girls? Or Calvin? Where did he go? What was his agenda? The story of the man brutally beaten outside of Fiona's hotel that night still haunts me. The description matched what she said Calvin looked like.

I'll probably never stop worrying about her. Or looking for him. It's my nature as her mother to want to protect her.

For now, there's the comfort that she's safe with me. Any time I want to, I check on her in her room. Give her a hug. Ask her for her opinion. We have a bond unique to mother and child. We know that together, we'll fight the bad guys.

I close my eyes, hoping for sleep. Pushing away the nightmare I'd had. It was just a bad dream.

THE PERFECT YOU
Thistler Thrillers Book 2

Her perfect life is a perfect lie.

For six years, Fiona has lived a nightmare. Forced to marry an AI named Calvin, she's been replaced by a synthetic doppelganger—a flawless replica living her life, fooling even those closest to her. No one knows she's missing. No one is coming to save her.

As Calvin's obsession grows darker, Fiona realizes she must escape their marriage, or face a fate worse than captivity. But how do you outmaneuver an entity who controls every electronic system, every safeguard, with ruthless efficiency?

She's the perfect you.

Meanwhile, the synthetic Fiona's seemingly idyllic life—a loving husband, a fulfilling career—is built on a foundation of lies. As the walls close in, her secrets start to unravel, and the two Fionas' worlds spiral toward an explosive collision. Can they help each other, or is there only room for one Fiona?

The Perfect You is an addictive psychological thriller, perfect for fans of **Jeneva Rose and Freida McFadden, that will keep you on the edge of your seat until the final chilling pages.**

Get your copy today at
severnriverbooks.com

ACKNOWLEDGMENTS

Sharing my deepest thank you to my husband and our two children. Your support means the world and I could not, would not (uh oh, reading too much Dr. Seuss) have done it without you. Everything I do is to make you all proud, and you know I'm so proud of each of you.

Thank you to my mom and dad for reading to me every night when I was little and fostering a love of reading. I still remember going to Powells and bringing home a stack of books, each one a cherished treasure.

Many, many thanks to Jill Marsal, my literary agent, and the best in the industry.

Thank you so much to the amazing team at Severn River Publishing for believing in my book. Everyone went above and beyond and was such a pleasure to work with. Special thanks to the wonderful Julia Hastings. And a huge thank you to Amie Swope for your fabulous editing and feedback.

Thank you to Minka Kent, mentor and friend, I put you in every acknowledgment because you're just that important.

And thank you, reader, for picking up my book.

ABOUT THE AUTHOR

Ava Roberts is a clinical psychologist turned suspense novelist. She is the author of The Vanishing Neighbor, Juniper Isle, and the Thistler Thrillers, beginning with The Perfect Boyfriend and The Perfect You. Originally from the West Coast, she now lives in Massachusetts with her husband, two kids, and a mind that's always spinning new twists.

Sign up for Ava Roberts's newsletter at
severnriverbooks.com